WILD
PLUM
AT NIGHT

WILD PLUM
AT NIGHT

Jamie Wheelas

SUNSTONE
PRESS

SANTA FE
New Mexico

First Edition

Printed in the United States of America

Library of Congress Cataloging in Publication Data:
Wheelas, Jamie, 1939–
    Wild plum at night / by Jamie Wheelas.—1st ed.
        p.   cm.
    ISBN: 0-86534-049-8
    I. Title
PS3573.H419W55   1996
81`3' .54—dc20   96-3596
                                         CIP

Published by SUNSTONE PRESS
            Post Office Box 2321
            Santa Fe, NM 87504-2321 / USA
            (505) 988-4418 / orders only (800) 243-5644
            FAX (505) 988-1025

Wild Plum

They are unpitied from their birth
  And homeless in men's sight
Who love, better than the earth,
  Wild plum at night.

—Orrick Johns

ONE

Even before he had left the bar in Espanola, Martine realized he was dead drunk, but he didn't care. There was a certain comfort in this intoxicated state, in the fading light of the ending day and in the blue and purple darkness gathering in the folds and recesses of the mountains on either side of the highway that was now taking him toward Santa Fe, New Mexico's ancient capital.

Drunk? It didn't matter. If he managed to drive the next few miles he would find one of his favorite bars, perhaps Los Dos Tortugas, and he would drink some more. He could make it. His drunkenness did not lessen his skill at driving the somewhat battered and dusty Volkswagen. Alcohol was a way of shutting out the world, allowing him to watch it from a safe distance as people watch dangerous criminals through one-way glass in police stations.

But, there was one slightly disturbing thought pressing dimly into his drunken isolation: what if the state police stopped him? What would they say about a priest in his condition? What would the monsignor and the archbishop say about a priest who had to be bailed out of jail for DWI? What did it matter what they might say? He hadn't said Mass in days. In fact, he had been gone from his parish at San Carlo for two weeks and drunk most of time. He laughed as he told himself that he had been AWOL. Absent Without Leave from the Church, that is. But who cares. Soon he would be permanently absent, ousted, and he whispered aloud, half mockingly, "from the One, True, Holy, Catholic and Apostolic Church."

By now his letter of resignation from the priesthood had not only been read by the archbishop, but in all likelihood acted on by the archdiocesan office, he thought. They undoubtedly had issued a letter of censure, defrocking him—tossing him out of the church.

He tried to remember his canon law. What was it the church did when it read one of its priests out of holy orders, took away the priest's authority to consecrate the bread and wine? There was a ritual for this action, he thought to himself as he tried to recall the exact term for being condemned and fired by the church, but in his inebriated state he could only think of one word: anathema. That was it. They would utter anathema over him and he could envision the yellowed parchment, encrusted with the seal of the Archdiocese of Santa Fe, bearing the details of this action to the Vatican. He could see the Holy Father bending slightly forward by candle light to read the parchment's Latin script telling of his downfall; and before this imagined scene vanished in his mind, he could see the Pope moving his head slowly from side to side in sad disapproval over the fallen priest.

But what did it matter, he asked himself again. Everything that he once was, all the things that made up his life—all of this had been swept away in one single devastating instant, the instant when Martine dePaul realized who he really was. It shattered his world for the first time in his few, young years; and in the days following this terrible realization he had sunken into self-loathing, drinking non-stop to shut the world out. Now he was guiding the little car back from an afternoon of drinking in an out-of-the-way bar where they knew who he was and didn't care; or if anything, the drinking patrons, ranch-hands and Hispanics, actually showed him a sort of deference, feeling some added sense of importance, drawn from being able to drink in the company of the amiable young "man of the cloth" from the church at Pueblo San Carlo.

That was it. They knew who he was, not what he was. Had they known the latter, even vaguely suspected it, he reasoned, they would have shunned him, perhaps even turned violent. Although he had been assigned to the archdiocese for less than a year, he knew the ways of these people and their deeply held intolerance for things they did not understand or accept.

"Yeah, Padre," bellowed one of the big cowhands as he threw a rough arm around Martine's shoulders back at the bar, "I don't care what folks say about Catholics, or that you are an Indian lover and live with those Redskins, you are good people. Don't let anybody tell you differently."

Only Martine was able to tell himself differently. What they saw was an uncomplicated facade that liquor helped build. He could match them drink for drink, beat them at shuffle board, or lose to them on the pool tables and hold their attention with imaginative small talk, but this was not the real Martine dePaul. This was not even the priest at San Carlo. This was someone, he discovered after many rounds at the bar, he could create at will and make believable and able to survive in a quite different world. But whoever this person was, he was not the real Martine.

The real Martine, he told himself starkly, had taken part in evil and had allowed it to influence and direct his life. In fact, it had possessed him and he had come to desire it, even lust after it. He thought fleetingly of a sermon on evil that he had once preached at San Carlo. "We agonize over what is wrong with our world," he had told his congregation, "and we search for answers and seek to place blame. We overlook the simple truth and don't want to believe it in our modern world. There is such a thing as evil. It still exists. Man still does evil and this is at the heart of most of the pain and suffering in our society today."

Could he have believed then that only in so short a time he himself would be a willing participant? He had been an instrument of evil and it had taken from him the world in which he had once lived a serene, happy life; and now that familiar world had been placed beyond his reach. It might as well be the Eden that was taken away from the original sinners, Adam and Eve, he thought, because now what was once his world existed in another dimension from which he had been expelled and there was no way back, all entry being barred as if by an avenging angel. This thought anguished his heart, bringing to him an almost unfamiliar sensation, grief. It clutched at his throat, brimmed upward in his being, leaving the salty sting of tears on his face.

The road ahead of him came fleetingly into clear focus. It was getting dark. The distant lights of Santa Fe twinkled here and there in the gathering gloom, more pronounced where it mingled with the swelling black shadows of the Jemez Mountains off to Martine's right. To his left, ponderous thunderheads, still reflecting streaks of color from the sun that had set far into Arizona, towered over the Sangre de Cristo Mountains.

Martine could not shake the thought of his lost world. In fact, he did not want his mood to change. His mind, honed by the afternoon of liquor, was sharply candid with itself, wanting the perverse pleasure that could be found in self-pity. He thought of Houseman's lines about the special world of youth that adults sometimes find they have lost, and he ruefully mouthed the poet's words aloud:

"That is the land of lost content,
 I see it shining plain,
The happy highways where I went
 And cannot come again."

His sense of loss had now taken on a bitter-sweet, not entirely unpleasant sensation, something akin to the feeling of nostalgia when one remembers sorrowfully a lost golden time, and in so remembering feels yet a tinge of that vanished happiness.

How clearly the alcohol made him see! In mentally observing himself, it was like that vantage-point given a viewer who might stand on the mountain tops on either side of him. The alcohol, he felt, helped him focus so he could cut through the obstacles of denial and see things as they really were: clear and crystal-like. In this way he could see without doubt or contrary rationalization what he truly was. He hated what he saw, and it gave him release to cry out in the silence around him. "Oh God, what did I ever do unknowingly and in my youth, what offense did I commit against you or some fellow human being that I should be punished with this affliction. And why should it be the cruelest affliction of all—one that puts me at odds with You in whom I have always believed. Why have You meted out this bitter portion to thy servant?"

At the core of this anguish was the knowledge that Fr. Martine Michael dePaul, Holy Order of St. Francis, and at twenty-six one of the most youthful priests of the ancient order ever to be assigned his own parish, had broken his vows in less than a year after having sworn on the Altar of God that he would renounce forever the allure of the world of flesh and walk in the footsteps of the Saint of Assisi the path of poverty, chastity and obedience.

∎

Hampton Court stood on the highest hill, if it could be called a hill because it was more like an imposing rise in the earth's surface, in the Hamptons of Long Island. With thirty-two rooms, not counting the guest and servants' quarters, it was a palace, really, and Edgar dePaul fancied his magnificent home as just that. After acquiring the three-story, white-columned mansion, he promptly christened it Hampton Court, after the royal retreat so beloved of Queen Anne and her courtiers who fled there to escape London's summer heat and idle away their days on the banks of the Thames. After all, as the head of a financial empire, chairman of the board of Allied Industrial Bank of Manhattan, dePaul considered himself and others at his level to be the nation's only legitimate claimants to royalty.

"We are the power," he would proclaim after several scotch and sodas brought his usual mirthless nature to a convival level. "Not presidents and congressmen, not governors, but the people who control the money have the power to make things happen. Most of us are not motivated by desire for power and acquisition. We serve the public and make better the lives of ninety percent of the people in these United States. We finance the great universities, the hospitals, the museums,the symphonies and opera companies. What blue collar worker, or what farmer, or what small town merchant, or what combination of these people, ever gave a library—even so much as a bookshelf—for the betterment and pleasure of their neighbors, their city or their state?" Then after an awkward pause in which none of his listeners would volunteer an answer, Edgar, his face reddened by drink and the intensity of his belief, would deliver his own thunderous answer: "None has because they can't afford it. They will never be able to afford it, not in a million years. After all, they are as far along in life as they want to be and they are only at that level because we, a handful of financiers and industrialists, provide the means—the jobs and the opportunities. We have made it possible for the mass of people to live in a comfortable, even luxurious style that they, by themselves and with their limited abilities and ambitions, could never have achieved."

Edgar dePaul would interrupt his declamation only when the servant announced dinner, and then he would proudly lead his guests to the gilded dining room. There over lobster thermidor and Long Island boiled corn, under the frowning gaze of dePaul ancestors frozen in ornate frames, he would continue with his theme about how society prospered and thrived because of the charity made possible by the corporate world.

"Take your average Joe Sixpack out there," he would spout. "He works for you and me. He has an average house in Bay Shore or Manhasset or wherever, but even so he lives better than any king or emperor ever did. Louis XIV lived at Versailles and it took hundreds of servants just to provide him with such creature comforts as ice for his drinks, white fish from the North Sea for his dinner, hot water for his bath and cool or warm air for his bedroom. Today, Joe Sixpack has all that and more and can't claim one servant to his name. Modern technology, made possible by business and industry, has given it to him, all in a package that fits into his average house. He presses a button and it's air-conditioned in his Bay Shore house, even on the hottest day. He presses another and his dinner is cooked, or there is instant entertainment from around the world on his living room TV. A short drive to the supermarket and he can bring back the most exotic food imaginable from any point on the globe.

"In this respect, he lives even better than Old Louie. Who has made this possible? We have, and we've thrown in free public education, cradle to the grave medical insurance, vacations and retirement besides. We are why the United States is great, and friends, we've even made it possible for most of the nations around the world to live in plenty and enjoy luxuries their grandparents never dreamed of. To put it bluntly, ours is the Kingdom and the Power, and it has produced the greatest civilization ever known to man. When the Good Book talks about only the few earning the right to enter in, we are that few. We have served millions of people, many of them often ungrateful or undeserving, but we have never complained about the freeloaders and the takers. Then, realistically, there's no way to separate them out from the deserving—divide the sheep from the goats as it were. The benefits from our labor, investments, imagination and enterprise fall on the good and bad alike. But make no mistake about it, we are the new royalty, the annointed few."

It was at Hampton Court that Martine dePaul, the only child of Edgar and Isadora dePaul, grew up, surrounded by nannies and servants and every extravagance that great money can bestow upon the only offspring of powerful and prominent parents. The great house had dominated his teenage years except when he was away at Groton, the preparatory school for the privileged and intelligent sons of the "ruling class" as Edgar liked to think of his family. Of course there were days, even as much as a week or two during inclement winter weather or when he had some special project to pursue, when Martine had lived in town—as he called New York City—in the family's apartment. But always Hampton Court, his circle of like-minded friends and his sail boat at the Manhasset Yacht Club lured him back to what he called "the country." When he thought seriously about himself, who he was and where he belonged in time and space, "The Court" was his being, his sanctuary—physically, and even spiritually.

It was a safety factor, he told himself. There he didn't have to deal with the world. There were no threats. He was safe. Safe from what, he didn't know. Nothing he could place his finger on threatened him, made his way of life at risk in any way. Yet, in his innermost self there was a vague uneasiness, a faint anxiety; but it took only a night of relaxation and a good sleep at "The Court" to make his world right again.

Martine turned seventeen during his last year at Groton, and this was a crucial year by his reckoning. One day he pulled aside the veil of superficial learning, all linked to what seemed a meaningless system of grades and honors for the superior student, and glimpsed an unbelievably rich world of art, philosophy and learning. It was something, he realized, that had been there all along, but like an invisible dimension it had surrounded him without his being aware of it. With only the first glimpse to guide him, he stepped into this new world and closed the door behind him, never looking back to see how that door had dissolved into the wall, leaving no seam at all. There now would be no turning back, ever. He would pursue literature, poetry, painting, music, philosophy, history and the sciences. He would read, he would study the masters and the classics and come to understand the world. This was a simplistic approach to the direction his life should take, he felt, but nonetheless it was a real goal—more important than the ephemeral, surface things he had reveled in most of his life: soccer and tennis, pulp novels, adventure movies and rock music. He realized that these were not ingredients of an important life and they never had been. If anything, they were among the priorities of people who lived on the surface, took from life and gave nothing back and beyond that could find no profound reason for their existence.

As far as Martine was concerned, that reason was the goal of life, and he knew that even with this first teenage epiphany he was still far from unraveling the secret, finding an answer. To fathom the reason for being, he now believed, he had to learn everything he possibly could about life; and, in turn, this left him only one course to follow: study life with dedication by reading the written word, the written record of men's experiences and their reflections. Martine did not expect his parents would understand. In fact, this wasn't something he could even discuss with his closest friends. Such topics could easily get him labeled as someone who was somehow different, not "one of us."

The possibilities were exciting, an adventure. The unexpected appeared with the opening of every new book, the turn of every page or in each new class that he would be taking in college. Yes, there would be a balancing act involved but it would not be a difficult feat. He would pursue his quest as an inward thing of the mind, while his outward being, his attitude, his demeanor would remain unchanged as far as his family and friends were concerned. It also would be a harmless deceit.

Martine suspected that countless people lived lives of quiet deception as he loved to paraphrase Thoreau's observation that most "men lead lives of quiet desperation." Their deception, he believed, amounted to nothing more than protecting their inward being from such scrutiny as might create misunderstanding and attract unwarranted criticism. They might talk a good game of baseball with friends and acquaintenances while having little if any real interest. This was their way of throwing others off the trail that might be taken with opera or the study of classical French literature, or even one of the sciences such as astrophysics. He was convinced there was no harm in this type of deception. It was like a social game the people in his life could not be allowed to win and thus endanger his his peace of mind.

Martine could only imagine the protest that would come from his father if he were to announce: "I have decided to seek the purpose of life."

"Good God, boy, aren't you old enough yet to have figured that out? Your purpose is to become successful—damned successful so that you'll be telling others what to do, not them telling you. That's the only way you ever get control of your life and that's what it's all about. When you have control, when you are in control you can make things happen, create, build. That's what we're put on this earth for. I have taught you this all your life, and now it's disappointing to hear you say you want to find out what life is all about, what your purpose is.

"I want you to train in business and banking, and once you have that degree you will join me—not at the top but at the bottom and work your way up just like I did; and then you'll find out who you are and what life is all about so quickly it will make your head spin. Yes sir, you won't know what hit you!"

Martine had heard this speech, or variations on it, a thousand times, he thought. No, there could be no dialogue with his father. It would just start the discourse again—just like when the subject of college came up. It began before Martine announced that he, like Edgar, would attend Cornell. In fact the university had been courting him since his junior year at Groton. Not only was he the son of a distinguished (and rich) alumnus, but he was distinguished in his own right through his scholarship and academic record, ranking at the head of his class. If his son's achievements pleased Edgar, he made no comment. Silence usually meant that he was happy or at least pleased. When Martine's mother had brought up what she considered her husband's indifference to their son's academic excellence, Edgar had blustered: "Why in the name of Heaven should I praise him for what he is expected to do? What he is achieving is for his benefit. He is the one who will profit from it. You know, that is precisely what is wrong with the world today: everyone expecting praise for doing what they know is their duty."

So, when making his announcement about Cornell, Martine mistakenly identified his major subjects: literature and history; and this had prompted the first of many outbursts from his father.

"Why in the world would one pursue a sissy line of study? Poems and absurd stories about ridiculous characters prancing around in lace panties and caught up in improbable situations that bear no resemblance to the real world; and history—a recitation of mankind's mistakes, most of them caused by a bunch of blockheads who didn't have the faintest idea how to make a dime. All these pansy writers, historians and looney philosophers were leeches on society who never produced anything of value for themselves or those around them. They didn't know how to contribute to a business world, how to promote capitalism. That's the very reason they were engaged in sissy pursuits in the first place. They didn't know anything else; and you want to be like that?"

Martine eventually avoided discussing his studies with his father. Edgar showed no sign of lessening his aversion to his son's academic direction, so he talked about every other aspect of university life at Ithaca, but he knew his father's disapproval was always just under the surface. After all, a report of his grades and academic standing was mailed by the university every semester to his parents, so he knew his father was well aware of the nature of his studies. His mother, on the other hand, was delighted with Martine's progress and made a point of carefully filing all of her son's grade reports.

By nature Martine was a cheerful person. In his childhood Isadora and family friends rarely mentioned it, but always thought of Martine as a "child of happiness." Sunlight seemed to fill his face and his smile emanated from deep within his spirit. It was never artificial and rarely failed to appear. More imporant, it was infectious. Sometimes Isadora feared her son's happy nature that so charmed everyone hid a vast shallowness in his spirit, perhaps even in his intellect It did not seem natural for a little boy never to cry, never to have a surly moment when denied some important wish or desire and never to know a few occasions when the shadows of pensive or fearful thoughts would appear on his face. Yet, there was always that light radiating from his very being. Isadora sensed that Martine must be totally unaware of how to do wrong, or think evil or even innocently injure people around him. There were never problems of disobedience or discipline; and her worry about shallowness was lessened somewhat as the boy quickly grasped philosophical and spiritual concepts. She had been shocked when at four years old he held up a tiny finger to interrupt her story and say brightly, "Ah, that's an idea instead of a fact."

The suspicion about shallowness, though, continued to nag her until at last she privately broached the matter with Father Patrick Joseph Monahan, the priest at St. Catherine's, the dePaul's family church. "I know this may seem silly, Father," Isadora said, "but isn't so much quote-unquote 'sweetness and light' in a child Martin's age a departure from the normal?"

"Isadora, my dear, dear Isadora," Father Patrick replied in an almost tut-tuting tone of voice, "have you never heard of innate goodness? I have known Martine since I baptised him and have watched him grow. He never misses confession and he loves the Mass. I have watched him out of the corner of my eye, and I would be willing to wager that he already knows the service by heart.

"But the point is, Isadora, you and Edgar are blessed. This child not only loves God, but God loves him. From birth he has been touched by God, destined to be a good person, perhaps even a holy person one day. With Martine, you see, he does not have to work at being a good and caring human being. It's not like with the rest of us who have to work at it every day of our lives. He has been touched by God, he has been given a gift from God—goodness and grace, pure unadulterated goodness of spirit. Oh, Isadora, do you realize how rare such a gift is and what it could mean to humanity and the church one day?"

Father Patrick then placed his arm around Isadora, seeing that she appeared to be intimidated by his revelation, and as he walked her toward his office door, he laid an index finger against his lips as he admonished, "But this gift is so precious, so much rarer than gold or any jewel that we could imagine, that you must never mention it, never reveal to anyone, not even Edgar, what we have discussed. This knowledge would make the enemies of God your child's enemies and we cannot have that. His gift will make itself known in time. Heaven only knows this is needed in our world of sorrow and misery and crime."

As Isadora and the priest parted, neither of them could have envisioned that Father Patrick would touch many thousands of lives as a future cardinal of the church.

Martine finally grasped the purpose for his life without realizing he was doing so. Looking back, he could not quite pinpoint the day it happened, but it was during his final year at Cornell. It didn't suddenly crystallize in his consciousness, but came gradually into his thinking almost the way a distant scene comes into focus as one adjusts a pair of binoculars. He came to know that he must place his life in the service of others as a dedication of himself, as a calling from God.

Little wonder that he drew the ultimate conclusion: He would enter the seminary and train as a priest after his graduation. The one thing he would delay to the very last would be breaking the news to his father, no inspired devotee of the Roman Catholic Church. He attended services on what he called "state occasions" and made sizable contributions and thought of them as "business expenses," but that was as far as religion went for him.

Martine had attended Mass almost daily and for a very different reason than his father's. In Ithaca he had found the little Church of the Transfiguration at the beginning of his freshman year and was drawn there more and more, especially to morning Mass at six before classes. There he found the tranquility and inward peace that sustained him through the day, giving him a boost mentally and physically so that no matter how vexing the day's tasks and problems, he rarely felt tired.

On those occasions when he spent a good portion of the evening with friends discussing philosophy over beer and pizza in one of the city's out-of-the-way bistros he could appear the next day rested as though he had enjoyed a good night's sleep. His close friends often marveled at his endurance but he never shared with them what he considered was his source of strength—a daily measure of spiritual conditioning. This was his secret.

Not only might they misunderstand this aspect of his life, but it was something so intensely personal that he could not frame it in words that would not sound maudlin or perhaps even unnatural. Parts of this guarded religious life were strange. For example, his emotional reaction to the prayer of consecration during the Mass. Why did its truth and beauty move him to tears, a sensation he almost never experienced otherwise? He reasoned that knowing and feeling the presence of Jesus Christ in the church was perhaps the most profound happiness that a human being could know, but why should such sheer beauty elicit tears? Could this be a sin of aestheticism, the worship of beauty rather than God? he wondered briefly, but put the question aside, concluding that any feeling so profound must come from his very spirit. He was doing what John had commanded in the Gospel: he was worshipping God "in spirit and in truth." But for now, though, the mysterious areas of his religious experience would remain part of his secret.

Surrounding his outward, every-day life was the grandeur of Cornell and the joy he found in living and learning there. He sometimes thought of the physical setting of the great university as a cathedral to delight the intellect. With a friend or by himself, he never tired of asorbing the splendor of this shrine of learning with its deep, wild ravines and bridges; the forest-covered hills falling away to the sparkling waters of Lake Cayuga; and all of it seen through a sort of mistiness that seemed to shroud it as a special sanctuary in time where the mind and spirit could be enriched while shielded from the rude intrusions of the outside world.

Sometimes, when he thought about it, Martine felt that no one could pass through Cornell's portals without being changed. He saw it as a catalyst that enriched the human spirit to greater charity while giving the mind the scope needed to be tolerant toward all men.

Martine's time to emerge from the university came rapidly and this also meant that the day of reckoning with his father was upon him. During the Christmas vacation he found he could put it off no longer. His father forced the issue by proclaiming at one of the many dazzling parties of the Hamptons' season that after graduation and a short vacation in Europe, his son would be off and running as one of his bank's newest team players.

Martine reserved a place of special distaste for the team-player cliche that vocabulary-improverished people in the business world liked to substitute for the simple word "cooperation." He saw the expression as demeaning because in its strictest definition it deprived employees of their individuality and creativity. If the expression did nothing else, however, it spurred him to the showdown with his father when they returned home that evening. It also guaranteed there would be little peace on earth during this Christmas at Hampton Court.

He invited Edgar and Isadora into the library, a place he somehow imagined vaguely intimidating for his irrepressible father. After they were seated near the fire, Martine, still standing, made his announcement abruptly.

"Mom, Dad, I won't be going into banking. I'm sorry, Dad, if by my silence I've misled you, and no disrespect intended, but I just have no interest in banking and business. I have applied to the seminary and they have conditionally accepted me for enrollment next June, shortly following graduation. I will study toward becoming a postulant and eventually a priest in the Order of St. Francis."

Only the crackling in the fireplace broke the stunned silence for what seemed like an eternity during which Edgar's face turned deep red. "What the hell do you mean, boy? What kind of foolishness have those damned priests pumped into your head? What sort of future can you offer yourself with this church business—all those men running around in their black dresses and begging everyone for a handout?" He paused, then blurted out. "I can't believe my son, who could have anything he wants in this world, except perhaps the British throne, would channel his life into something that offers nothing but a dead end—absolutely no opportunity, no reward, nothing, zilch! I see the fine handiwork of that damned Patrick Monahan in this. He has done nothing but take from this family ever since he was a priest, and especially now that he is a cardinal or whatever kind of bird it is. Maybe it's a vulture because he wants to take my son...why that SOB...that...!"

"Now, Edgar, dear," Isadora said with a nervous but soothing smile. "You wrongly accuse Pat. I'm sure he had nothing to do with Martine's decision. Besides, it's an honor for our family that the church would choose our son for a life of service."

"Dad, Dad," Martine interjected quickly before his father could roar on, "this is the most important future ever offered any human being—a chance to help others, to make life better on this planet."

"Well, I know a little bit about the Bible, boy, and I believe it says that the Lord helps those who help themselves; and that's the best advice that your parasites, who want all that help, can follow, and the church, too, for that matter. That's the way they can make life better for all of us on this earth—get out and do a good day's work and earn a paycheck."

"Dad, try to understand my decision. It's more than just helping others. This is also service to God." But even as he spoke the words, Martine knew such a concept was unacceptable to his father. It was something he rejected so completely that it might as well be the doctrine of some obscure cult of sun worshippers.

"I think it's about time God did a little support work in his own kingdom," Edgar said disgustedly. "He needs to invest in His own stock and build some capital, instead of expecting everyone else like my son to take all the risks."

"Edgar!" said Isadora in a hushed but horrified voice.

"I mean it," said Edgar. "I am tired of people like myself doing all the giving, paying all the taxes and supporting all the righteous and worthy causes, civic do-gooders and church panhandlers in this world; and now they want my son. Enough is enough. They figure that by getting Martine, they can come in the back door and get all of it one day when I kick off and everything I possess goes to the boy. That means it would go to the church. It's one and the same thing if he becomes a priest, and damned if I'm going to sit here and see that happen."

Martine wasn't sure what his father meant by this implied threat and he wasn't going to ask. This much seemed clear: the more he tried to explain, the more annoyed his father was becoming.

There was no way he could mollify his father into accepting his intended course. Even if he could be successful in persuading his father not to verbally protest, the elder dePaul's mental objection would remain. This made Martine remember the lines from Samuel Butler:

> "He that complies against his will
> Is of his own opinion still."

Martine knew it would be better to let the matter drop for the time being. Perhaps it was a cruel thing for a parent to be denied a son in this manner, denied the chance for posterity. Martine did not want to hurt his father. He reasoned that such parental desires as these were, after all, human foibles; and if there was hurt it would be eased by time.

This impasse illustrated to Edgar dePaul that there were two things his money could not buy. All his life he had boasted that there was only one exception: "Money can buy all but one thing. It can buy love, friends, power, social position and even justice; but it cannot buy talent. Unfortunately, you have to be born with that." Now he was learning that money also could not buy his son's choice of a future.

∎

"This is about the boy, isn't it?" asked Cardinal Monahan after he and Isadora were seated in her drawing room.

"Well, yes it is, in part," said Isadora, caught off guard by the sudden directness. "But since when can't I have you to dinner without having an ulterior motive, Pat? I have several things I would like to discuss with you. Some good news, in fact; and I'm just as happy that Edgar is out of town. You know, he blames you for Martin's choosing the seminary and the priesthood, and he can be very unreasonable."

"There's not much chance that I would forget Edgar's bad nature when it comes to certain topics," said Monahan. "I understand his position, in part, and appreciate how he feels. As we both know, he was bent on Martine stepping into his shoes at the top one day. It was a matter of pride with Edgar. He wanted his success to live on in Martine and he wanted the world to see this and give him credit for it.

"Now Edgar's pride has been hurt and when this happens to a man like Edgar you can expect him to lash out, maybe get even in some emotional way. But give him time. This may heal if Edgar, in his own mind, can forgive the church and that might just happen when he sees how happy Martine is in parish work."

"I don't know, Pat. He's awfully bitter. I shudder to think how he may react the first time Martine shows up here wearing a collar." Now Isadora's usually kindly face was dark for only a moment as she prepared to share her thoughts. "I wasn't going to approach this first, but since you brought up the matter of Martin's assignment, I have a request that my son wishes me to share with you. He says that if anyone outside of the Holy Father himself can bring this about, you can. Martine wants parish work, but in an area as remote and distressed as possible. He not only wants to work for the spiritual needs of people but he wants to join them in fulfilling their material needs on the land—planting and harvesting food, finding modern techniques to solve problems such as producing water and sanitation for them.

"Oh, Pat, I'm afraid he hopes for a very large plate and the means to fill it to capacity. Is there any place that fits this description? Is there such a parish in the United States?

"Sad to say, Isadora, there are dozens of such parishes in our country. They are the parishes where the church has had to assume almost every role of government: providing food, water, health services and even education. We have such places right here in the Diocese of New York. There just isn't enough money or enough trained people to go around; but, I think what Martine has in mind is getting close to the land and with basic, simple people—an Indian reservation somewhere, perhaps in New Mexico."

"I've been in New Mexico—once years ago. I think it was in Santa Fe. Outside of the few wealthy individuals I met, I got the impression there was great need among the people in general. Someone talked me into stopping over there to attend the opening night of some local opera company."

"Yes, there are Indian pueblo churches where Martine's great talents and capacity for work would be welcomed with open arms by the archbishop, Gallegos, I think it is. But stress to Martine that we are talking about nothing short of a foreign country and a totally different way of life out there."

The cardinal turned and beamed a broad smile as he spoke to his hostess, using the name only Edgar and a few intimates were permitted. "You see, Izzy, that wasn't so difficult, now was it? In all honesty, however, I must make a confession. I have talked with Martine's advisors several times. They have kept me informed of his excellent religious and academic progress. So I have already been paving the way and Martine will be in the Land of— what's that state's nick-name? Enchantment, that's it, before the ink dries on his letters of transfer."

"Oh, Father Pat," Isadora cried. "How can I ever thank you? Martine will be in your debt forever. In your own way you have served as two fathers, spiritual and temporal, to our son."

Cardinal Monahan held up a wavering finger to silence Isadora's enthusiasm as he put down his coffee cup. "There's more," he continued. "If after a year Martine sees his assignment out there in an untenable light, warts and all, and feels he mistakenly accepted this challenge, then he shall be transferred back to this diocese and to a place on my staff until he gets his bearings.

"Isadora, we talked years ago when he was a child, you'll remember, and I told you of my secret discovery that Martine was a special child of God. Now, that he has reached manhood, I know now more than ever that he has been touched by God and that his life is motivated by the kind of grace we other mortals only dream and pray for. I am convinced that the hand of God protects him from evil in this world.

"So just for the sake of argument, let me play the devil's advocate and ask how is it fair that one person, even without asking, is given the grace of God for no reason to protect him from sin and all evil, while we throngs of others toil and beg just for a little crumb of grace to help us in the fight against the powers of evil?"

Cardinal Monahan turned to Isadora with a fervent look. "Don't misunderstand, Izzy, but you see my point? That's why Martine is special, and I believe that only you and I are fully aware of his special status and that's the way it must remain.

"As far as Martine is concerned, I stand on the heights of expectancy. What will come from him? What miracle, what revelation that will open the eyes of people? I know it is there...something wonderful and yet terrifying. Even little children in the street stop their play and follow him."

Isadora and the cardinal turned almost at the same instant to gaze at the photo of Martine encased in a gold frane standing on the desk. A handsome young man with a crew-cut smiled out at them, his deep blue eyes full of the joy of living, a face that reassured beholders that there was still goodness in the world.

"And now to the real reason for our meeting, Cardinal Pat," said Isadora as she poured another steaming cup of coffee. "It is my surprise for you and I shan't be as tricky as you in breaking the good news about Martine. It is my pleasure to assure you that I have found a way to finance your proposed half-way house in Manhattan—all $2.5 million of it."

"I am humbled and overwhelmed," said the cardinal, stunned. "That's incredibly splendid, Izzy. But what about Edgar?"

"He'll never know how I came by the funding, so don't ask, Pat," she said smiling.

∎

Night had covered Santa Fe as Martine slowly parked the Volkswagen at Los Dos Tortugas. Garish neon signs in the windows between the lounge's closed blinds and the outside window glass advertised "Corona Cerveza," a popular Mexican beer, and "Coors Made With Rocky Mountain Spring Water." The ever-present red chili ristras hung from the building's vigas that protruded through the lounge's walls. Further back, suspended against the adobe surface were hangings of Indian corn in various colors.

Although he wore blue jeans and a sweater—never a collar—when he came in, he had been identified long ago by the staff as "the padre from San Carlo." Martine was astonished at how quickly the word got around, even to people he didn't know; but then many of his parishioners came to this neighborhood bar and he had quickly discovered that Hispanic and Indian people were more sensitive to the presence of "church people."

Stepping inside to the blare of mariachi music, Martine vaguely heard someone calling. It was Poncho, the bartender who was well known for his command of languages. He could talk to his clients in English, Spanish or any one of the Indian dialects. "Hey, Padre," he called again. "I have a message for you. It seemed urgent."

Martine suddenly felt clear-headed now that the edge of the afternoon's drinking had worn off.

"First, Poncho, give me a beer. I need it. I've had a hectic afternoon." Martine wondered why he had said that. He had not had a hectic time. Actually it was a relaxing five or six hours that took his mind off the problems eating into his heart and soul.

Martine took a deep drink from the heavy foam-topped stein Poncho handed him. "Now," he said in a humorous, half-wise voice, "what's so urgent?"

"You got me," said Poncho. "An Indian boy brought this note and said it was for you. I think he was from San Carlo."

"Was he a nice-looking kid, about sixteen, and standing about this high?" said Martine, measuring with his outstretched hand five and a half feet off the floor.

Poncho glanced up from his bar tasks and nodded. "That would be Taegu. He works for me," Martine added. "He does odd jobs around the church and my apartment. He's a sharp kid."

Martine looked down at the folded paper and noticed with a sharp pang of surprise that it was not a note at all. It had the letterhead and seal of the Archdiocese of Santa Fe. Its message, however, was note-like in its brevity: "The archbishop wishes to see you immediately. Please call and make an appointment at your earliest convenience." It was signed by the chancellor, Monsignor Montoya.

TWO

San Carlo was unusually quiet. Only the bells of San Luis Rey Church came alive as the faintest early light heralded the sunrise over the distant Sangre de Cristo Mountains above New Mexico's capital city.

Father Martine dePaul opened his eyes slowly to guage the intensity of light and closed them to see himself in the darkness of self as he murmured his never-failing morning prayer that followed his making the sign of the Cross over his chest. Although the words were always the same, the prayer was heartfelt, starting with: "In the name of the Father, the Son and the Holy Spirit. God, thank you for bringing me safely through the night; and lead me safely through this day. In the name of the Father, the Son and the Holy Spirit. Amen."

As with most all days that had gone before in his twenty-six short years, or at least as far back as he could remember, there was a special reason to be alive on this day. Anticipation filled his being as he thought about the coming Mass that would echo in ancient San Luis Rey Church. This was the one constant in his life and from it flowed all else: joy, elation, contemplation, strength and endurance. It shaped and defined the boundaries of his life. Nothing else—the taste of food, the comfort of shelter or the quenching of thirst—gave him such delight, bordering sometimes on ecstasy. Participation in these ancient rites transcended everything. In the Mass, in its ritual, in its meaning and in its mystery were all the things that mattered to Martine, or that should matter to any other human being, he felt. He marveled at the effect it had on his mind and spirit; but then that was how it was supposed to be, else why could elements of the Mass be described as "these Holy Mysteries"?

Martine had heard the church bells being rung by his helper, Taegu. This meant he had just about twenty minutes to shower (he would shave when he returned for the breakfast he usually shared in his kitchen with Taegu), throw on jeans and a sweater, stride the hundred yards in the open to the vestry from his apartment in the church complex and get vested for the Mass. He knew that as usual the air outside would be bracing because from his studio's single large window he could see the belt of snow left by the now departed winter above the Santa Fe ski basin, although spring had brought tender green leaves to the cottonwood trees on the mountain's lower slopes. He also could see that the pueblo village was stirring. Smoke from burning piñon was coming from many chimneys in the gray dawn and here and there several women were in their yards preparing the fires in their horno ovens for the day's bread baking. The sweet, pungent piñon smoke was already bringing a welcomed aroma to his fairly snug adobe and brick apartment.

He remembered Cardinal Monahan calling New Mexico a foreign country. That it was, and in some respects it was as remote from modern America as the world described in James Hilton's *Lost Horizon*. Just as with the people in the Himalayas, Martine thought as he closed his apartment door, time didn't seem to matter much to the people here. If it took a year or ten years—especially with the older Indians and Hispanic people—what did it matter just so long as purpose or results were achieved? After all, this was an ancient land where people had established a civilization thousands of years before the Spaniards came and even their arrival was more than four hundred years ago.

Martine marveled when he thought about the village of San Carlo being many times older than New York where speed and efficiency were among the driving forces of most business and industry. There so many of the millions of people who worked to the drive of time had somehow lost their humanity, he thought. He conjured up an image he had once seen in a magazine photograph, of throngs of New Yorkers stepping without pause over a body on the steps of a subway entrance. Such indifference could never happen in San Carlo. These people were one with the elements of fire, land and water. Time was not their master. They were at peace with it.

Martine liked this concept. It made him feel as if he had been here forever, and the pace of living had slowed for him. He was not pressed to meet any deadline. Time seemed to be in his control and move with him. He could not imagine returning to live in New York or the Hamptons.

At the far end of the cobble stone walk, where it terminated at the main doors of St. Luis Rey, he could see Taegu in his white cassock, already dressed for acolyte service and pumping his arm up and down, meaning that Father Martine needed to walk briskly if the Mass was to begin on time. The open area in front of the church held a small cluster of vehicles, two of which Martine could identify. The battered pickup belonged to Avery Dalrymple, the Santa Fe artist and sculptor, who, irreverent though he was, faithfully drove the few miles out to serve as organist for the church without pay. Almost from the day the new priest arrived, they were able to communicate as if they had known one another for years. Dalrymple had a brilliant mind and could discuss knowledgeably any topic ranging from religion and the arts to the glories of classical French literature and the technical intricacies of geology. But, the artist also was a good listener and always ready with advice. Martine was grateful to have such an intelligent confidant.

Half in jest, perhaps, the organist had made it clear that he carried out his churchly duty so assiduously because he loved Bach and this was the only organ available for practice. Dalrymple's services weren't really necessary for a low, early-morning Mass, but he attended nonetheless to provide what he laughingly called "background" on the organ.

Father Fabian Chavez, an old grizzled Franciscan priest who lived alone in semi-retirement in a rambling old house filled almost to brimming with books, also proved a welcome discovery. Since the day of the Great Flood, Martine liked to say humorously, Father Fabian had kept every book that came into his possession and now the only space left in his home was on the tops of other book stacks covering every floor. There were only paths winding through the stacks and linking the kitchen, bedroom and living room. Long ago, radios, televison sets and non-vital furniture pieces had disappeared under the layers. The old priest had also assured Martine that he was quite at home in St. Luis Rey Church and would fill in whenever needed. "Just say the word," he added. The tone in his voice told Martine that this was a sympathetic ear waiting to hear any and all stories of spiritual need or distress.

Martine smiled as he noted the familiar white Jeep with an

elongated circular trademark containing three "Js" at the center. It was from the Three-J Ranch and had been driven in by the rancher Amanda Cameron and her daughter, Rebecca, regular communicants. His church, he found, was parish church to a number of ranch families who lived along the upper Rio Grande River and were neighbors to the San Carlo people. Amanda's husband, Tom, a leather-faced man who seldom spoke to anyone, attended services infrequently, insisting that duties on the vast Cameron ranch kept him mostly confined there.

Martine could hear the strains of "Jesu, Joy of Man's Desiring," coming from inside the church. He was glad this was a week-day service and not the full-blown High Mass of Sunday mornings and special saints days. These services required a lot of singing and a great voice was not one of his natural endowments.

The ritual at the special services had taken some getting used to because the pueblo people brought in their own ceremonial touches that included feathers and sacred tribal relics to accompany the procession, and the beating of ceremonial drums. He was not yet comfortable with this unusual bit of native embellishment that had existed since Spanish colonial days. The padres grudgingly tolerated the use of what they considered the pagan pageantry in order to persuade the native people to accept Catholicism. No one from the cardinal's office had advised, maybe the better word was fore-warned, him about this exotic ritual not only practiced in some parishes of the Archdiocese of Santa Fe, but officially condoned by the church itself. Martine rather liked these mysterious frills, but was thankful that guns were not fired as was the custom in some native parishes during celebration of the Mass.

Martine had only become fully aware of the congregation as he began to distribute the consecrated wafers. Passing down the row of communicants, dark-haired San Carlo women and one very elderly cacique with long, straight gray hair, he was soon in front of the Camerons. Something was very different about them today as their characteristic image of blonde hair and vital blue eyes pushed into his clearing vision. Instead of two, there were three of them standing before him to receive the Sacrament. In addition to Amanda and Rebecca, the young teenage daughter, there stood a tall, smiling young man, obviously a son because he had his arm placed protectively around his sister's shoulder.

The Camerons had never told Martine about a son, and while he had never seen the youth before, he knew without being able to explain it to himself that this was the case. This intuitive response startled Martine into an unaccustomed pause, nearly causing him to lose concentration; but collecting himself, he once again caught the ritual's rhythm and faced the young man who now smiled broadly as if ready to utter a greeting. Such a departure from the traditional somber look of his communicants embarrassed Martine and caused him to quickly look down.

Loss of poise was an emotion pretty much unknown to Martine. He hoped the Camerons had not noticed. It was important to Martine that the people in his parish approved of his performance and he would do nothing to cause them discomfort or prompt them to be critical. The shepherd must have the confidence and trust of his flock, he often told himself.

With the Mass concluded, Martine stood at the church entrance, greeting each of the thirty or so parishioners. In most instances he was able to call them by name and send a greeting home to their families. Among the last to leave were the Camerons, Amanda leading the way. Taking his hand and leaning forward to touch his cheek with her lips she said, "Oh Father Martine, I can't tell you how eagerly I have waited for this day because I have so much wanted you to meet our handsome son, Lance."

There was the laughing smile again. The young man exuded goodwill and friendliness, but Martine felt cautious about his new parishioner without being able to identify what it was that was disconcerting about the boy. Perhaps he was too forward, but then that was a style with many people in the West, he had found. A powerful arm and hand reached out and took Martine's and its touch was warm and curiously sensitive.

"Padre, you're all I've heard about since I got home, and I think you're going to be my kind of person—somebody that knows about something more than ranching and cattle. Finally, there's someone in my age group to talk with. If we aren't able to agree on every-thing, we have our age in common and a fresh view of the world to work from. I know we're going to enjoy talking."

"How old are you, Lance?" Martine asked.

"He's nineteen, acts fourteen and everybody thinks he's at least thirty," asserted Amanda, taking back the conversation.

"But," said Martine in a slightly hesitant tone, "you and Tom never mentioned having a grown son!"

"Well, Tom wouldn't," said Amanda with some exasperation. "He never tells anybody anything. He wouldn't have told me we had a son if there had been any way to avoid it. But there he is and he's home from college for the summer."

"Where do you attend school?" Martine asked.

Again Amanda answered for him as she said brightly, "He goes to the university in Albuquerque. We believe in a college education. Father Martine, possibly you didn't know that I graduated from school in Switzerland. Even Tom went, New Mexico Tech, and Rebecca here, wants to go to Wellesley. But I don't know about her going off to the East with so much crime and so many terrible things going on back there."

"Ah," said Martine, "you went to Switzerland to get a degree in a foreign language."

"No, my parents sent me to a proper girl's school run by nuns in Europe so I could get a degree in behavior away from boys," Amanda said laughingly. "But seriously, now, Father, we're so delighted you are here, and while I know you are involved in many duties and responsibilities with our church and the congregation, I want you and Lance to get to know one another. He needs an intellectual outlet and a church influence, and he can be so useful to you, showing you this part of the country. He grew up here, and he knows a lot of young people you would enjoy meeting. It's not good for you to be so cut off out here and away from people your age."

Martine smiled and made no reply. He was at once puzzled and a bit shocked by Amanda's apparent desire to create a friendship between the boy and himself. And he didn't need companionship. He was not lonely and certainly priests did not seek companions. They had friends, yes, but that was as far as it went. Besides, his church-community duties were keeping him occupied, well into the evenings at times, often returning home just in time to say his holy offices, shower and fall into bed.

"Hey, Padre," said Lance. "Mom's right. We're going to get together a lot this summer when things out at the Three-J lighten up a little. I'd buy lunch today, but I promised to get home and give Dad and our foreman a hand with some work up at the line camp in the mountains. Hey, I've got it. How about dinner tomorrow night? I'll pick you up about seven and we can try the Palace or the Gate of Spain. It's on me. They have great food and drinks."

Martine was becoming uncomfortable as he tried to think of some polite and prudent way to decline the invitation, yet wise heads in the church had advised him many times that politics and business were part of his responsibility. In fact, when he was briefed by Monsignor Montoya he had cautioned: "Many of the big ranching people are important contributors to the church—to the archdiocese. I'm not suggesting special favors for such parishioners, but do bear in mind they are the backbone of our effort here. In other words, Father Martine, all Catholics are equal in the eyes of the church, but some are a little more equal than others." There had been no humor in the chancellor's voice when he tendered this advice.

"Well, let me get back to my office and, and look over...."

"That settles it, then," said Lance with finality. "At seven sharp. I'll pick you up."

Once more Lance was shaking his hand, this time with both hands, and Amanda was waving back over her shoulder as she moved toward the Jeep with Rebecca in tow. It was too late, Martine could see. There was no gracious way of getting out of the dinner date. Perhaps he could phone out to the ranch, he thought, after going back to his office, and offer his apologies; but he could not think of any pressing duty demanding his time tomorrow evening. And no matter how desperate the situation, Martine would never consider telling a small white lie, no matter how small.

Back in the church office and occupied with a stack of uninspiring paperwork, Martine felt almost relieved when Taegu interrupted, coming in to report that he had completed his tasks for the morning.

"Taegu, do you know the Camerons, the family from the Three-J Ranch?" asked Martine. "You know, they were at Mass this morning?"

"Oh, yes, I've known them all my life," replied Taegu. "I worked out there last summer, but the pay wasn't much. That's why I'm working here before my senior year so I'll have a little more money."

"You know Lance Cameron, then. What's he like? Is he for real? I mean, is he on the up and up—the decent sort of guy he seems to be?"

"He's one loco Gringo, Padre."

"What do you mean by that, Taegu?

"Well, it's kinda hard to explain," said Taegu in a halting voice.

"He's a...what you call in English...you know, like someone who makes lots of hell?"

"Ah, you mean a hellion. What is it that he does?" Martine thought of the big smile Lance flashed during Mass.

"He drinks. You've never seen anyone put booze away like he can. He drinks sometimes for days without going home; and he drives—races is more like it. I don't know how many sport cars he has torn up and always comes out without a scratch. But, the big thing is that no one in their right mind would trust him with their sister. He thinks he's a stud, laying every girl he can in Santa Fe County."

"Do you know this first hand?" said an incredulous Martine.

"Well, no, Padre," said Taegu. "I have seen him drunk and roaring around in one of his cars, but I haven't actually seen him doing it. He's gotten several girls in the village pregnant, they say."

"Oh, no, no! I didn't mean to suggest you had seen him in the act," Martine explained. I just mean one has to be careful about repeating what people say about others. We have to be sure that what we are telling is true, factual. Remember that sin of bearing false witness against our neighbors?"

"Perhaps he's not so bad as they say," Taegu hastened to add. "Maybe old Lance is just wild, like Gringo people say. I need to go home now, Padre. Is there anything else you need done?"

After Taegu had departed, Martine leaned back behind his desk and pondered what might happen tomorrow evening with the "wild hellion" from Cameron Ranch. He smiled as he casually thought about the chances of making a conversion. Nothing was impossible as the biblical story of Saul of Tarsus illustrated. But of one thing Martine felt confident: he would get Lance to talk, reveal himself. Drawing people out was Martine's specialty.

∎

Clacking castanets and the sound of tapping toes filled the Gate of Spain as Clairita entertained with a plaintive flamenco story of Old Seville. One great window of the lounge section, where Martine and Lance were seated, looked out over a night-shrouded Santa Fe where the purple darkness sparkled with a thousand lights. Inside burning logs scattered their sparks in the fireplace, lit to take the chill off the spring night.

Martine was impressed. "This really is what some places in Spain are like," he mused. "A very faithful copy. How did you know I would like this?"

"Oh, that's not hard to figure out, Padre," said Lance, smiling and seeming to swell with pride over being found so clever. "You're a man of taste, Eastern Establishment and all that; several trips to the old world under your belt. I would expect no less from a man of such discernment and erudition."

Martine could tell that Lance was trying to impress him but he ignored this ploy and replied, "Yes, but I am also a person of simple tastes, and when you speak of the Establishment, that's my father, and I can assure you he would hate this place. I can hear him now: 'This is not American. What's the matter with these people?' He's absolutely xenophobic when it comes to dining out. Nothing foreign for him."

"That's just because he's older than you," said Lance knowingly. "And by the way, Padre, isn't it time I called you Martine?"

"Lance, I thought you knew to call me by my first name. I've never liked titles, anyway. And speaking of age, how is it they served you a drink and you're only nineteen? Isn't that against the law? Whoa, I'm guilty, too, because I'm an adult and I know you are under age, and to make it worse, I'm a priest of the church. Oh, boy!"

"Hold it, Padre, I mean, Martine! I'm drinking age. The legislature lowered the legal age to eighteen, but there is a big drive on by the Republicans to hike it back up to twenty-one; and they probably will, too. So, come down off the high altar. It's okay. And I might add I've been served drinks here and almost everywhere else since I was seventeen and no one has ever said a word. Here, they wouldn't mention it anyway...just isn't done." Amused at Martine's look of concern, Lance threw his head back and laughed heartily, shaking his tousled blond hair away from his eyes as he did so.

"So young and so serious," Lance continued, "but at least I'm glad you didn't wear the collar. That puts a damper on things."

"Lance, my lad, I'll have you know I earned that collar the old fashioned way," said Martine, joining in the laughter. "I worked for it...worked my way through the Vatican catacombs! That's how you get to be a Holy Roman Vampire!" Their vigorous laughter had an edge brought on by the drinks.

Martine liked his companion's laughter; but for all his adult ways he was still very much a boy and perhaps this evening was the opening Martine needed to begin redirecting Lance's energy, provided he was as wayward as the gossip indicated. Martine could think of nothing that pleased him more than the thought of having a mission. In fact, his very career was a mission designated, he believed down deep and secretly, by the Almighty. And what better place to begin than here at Pueblo San Carlo and with young people like Lance Cameron? He felt a sudden rush of happiness. Everything was on track, turning out just as he had so often envisioned.

"Martine, you're really okay, just like I told Mom you were," Lance said above the hum of the now crowded lounge. The waiter, dressed in an ancient Andalusian style garb, brought them another drink and Lance released their reserved table in the dining section when he learned they could be served where they were.

Martine moved into a more serious mode. "So, Lance, my boy, quo vadis? What direction do you want to see your life go? What are your goals?"

"I want to savor life, drink from it every last drop, leave nothing to be wasted by weeds and old age. I want to spend my most vigorous years making love, bedding all the most exotic and interesting women I can find, a life of wine, women and song, as they say."

"Isn't that a rather narrow, hedonistic view of your life in a world that needs so many things done by those like yourself who know how to do them?" asked Martine.

"Martine, we're talking about what I want for myself, not what I might be able to give the world. We're talking about just my needs and what makes me happy. You asked me what I wanted, and I'm telling you. Let me use the words of Ezra Pound:

'I'd rather have my love
    'Tho rose leaves die of grieving,
Than do high deeds in Hungary
    Past all men's believing.'

There. The quote may not be exact but that's what I mean."

Lance's smile faded when he saw the grave look on his dinner guest's face. "Oh, Martine, I see I've shocked you. Because of our ages, I forget what you are. My apology?"

"Come off that, Lance. I'm not shocked. I wear the collar around my neck, not around my brain. I know the desires and needs of vital young men. I'm aware what many of them do, how they live. I just question the morality of it and the reason—especially in an intelligent young man like yourself."

"Then, if we're being frank and nothing is off limits," said Lance with a knowing smile that came from only one side of his mouth, "what about yourself? Isn't making love the most wonderful thing you've ever felt, ever done? Wouldn't you want the ecstacy to be something that would last into eternity?"

"No," replied Martine emphatically. "There's only one ecstacy for me and that comes from the Blessed Sacrament."

"You mean," said a disbelieving Lance, "you've never had sex, never filled a woman with joy? Then, there's another part of your anatomy you've put that collar around. There I go, offending you again!"

"No, no, that's not it. You're missing the point, Lance. I am a servant of the eternal and living God, a servant of the church and as such, I am obedient only to their will, not to mine. My desires must be sublimated to a spiritual stage of love, the love of the everlasting possession of the good, as Plato might have said it."

"That's pretty deep."

"Okay, put another way: I have given my life to the church and the Kingdom of Heaven, and to serve the will of God with complete dedication, all things in that life—what would be a normal life—all the energies are converted to serving. That way there are no distractions from my effort to reach perfection in my service and to achieve good in this world."

"Good grief," said Lance, wincing, "that deprives you of love and leaves your life a hollow shell."

"Not at all," said Martine as he smiled. "The church is my love, the Kingdom of God is my life. Not only is it not hollow, it is the most complete life that any human being can know."

"Well, you've got to understand something, too," said Lance, his face somber. "I don't have your faith, Martine. I'm not sure I have any faith at all—at least I don't have enough that would empower me to give my life to an ideal as you are doing. And certainly I don't believe in some rule that says I can't make love and enjoy this body. Those rules were made up by men back at a time when they had whole harems of women, and they didn't want any young studs cutting in on their string. So they just declared it a sin for anyone who might have any ideas about dipping their wick in the harem."

"Let's take one thing at a time," said Martine. "Why do you have doubts about your faith?"

"Because...well, look, evolution is not a theory. It's a fact; and every day that passes we dig up more of the world that has existed for millions, even billions of years; and here's the Bible with this fantastic tale about how it was all created in seven days just by God saying something like Shazam! Come on, Martine, you've studied science and history and you know the world; you know the universe is billions of years old and that space and all the worlds beyond us in other galaxies extend on forever—through time and out of mind. What about your Garden of Eden tale, now, Padre?"

As he began his answer, Martine noticed that Lance was digging into his fettuccine and it looked like excavation work. "I don't have any argument with most of what you have said. Most of it is basically true. I think what causes all the misunderstanding and anguish here is the time frame, seven days. To God, the omnipotent and omniscient, what is a billion years? It's hardly a twinkling in time. I think the point that many people miss here is that God, like time, has always been and He always will be. He IS. In a very few of the bibical quotes directly attributable to Him, he says so. He says, 'I am.' He says further that he is Alpha and Omega, the beginning and the end. He says that He, the one God—who is the universe—IS.

"We know that in our science today. Einstein has shown through his equations that time doesn't pass. That's a human notion. Measurements of time have been recalculated and changed by man countless times, and in some parts of the world time still isn't measured by our standards. Time IS. God IS. What does that tell you? That the seven days of Creation could have been billions of years long. I think it's an even greater miracle that God worked through evolution to create us, our world. What an utterly breathtaking manifestation of his power—far more exciting than a world brought into being by magic tricks...Shazam! as you say.

"As for your Garden of Eden, what's wrong with that? Man does live in such a garden. Can you look at the Sangre de Cristos, or the Grand Canyon, or the Hudson Valley or the Great Lakes and tell me this earth is not a garden that we live in and are desecrating every day? So where else would you have had God put man in this world? What story would early, primitive minds have understood? They weren't equipped to deal with concepts like evolution or relativity. In fact, the Greeks used the same story and instead of Adam and Eve, we find Epimetheus and Pandora living in a garden. It took thousands of years just to get people—even the Holy Church—to comprehend the notion of a round Earth and a heliocentric world. The Garden of Eden, then, is one of the bibical writers' finest myths, truly inspired by God; and it is true in every respect.

"And to sum up...." said Martine bursting into laughter. "Hey, I really let you have it, didn't I? You didn't expect that."

Lance, deep in thought, realized the nature of Martine's examples and joined in the laughter. Showing that he appreciated Martine's dissertation, he leaned back and applauded lightly.

After a moment, Lance began a fresh drink and looked intently at Martine: "Tell me then, why all these 'Thou shalt nots'? Why is there forever someone in the church and in the Bible telling me how I ought to conduct my private life, what rules to follow, what sex I shall have and how much? What has my private life to do with the broader scheme of this world?"

"Well, a great deal, actually," replied Martine. "Man's individual conduct as opposed to the welfare of all men is a very complicated topic. First, let me say there are all kinds of religious laws that leaders, rabbis, prophets and others imposed on their people and these rules sometimes gradually became a part of religious practice. For example, the Jews and their Kosher rules pertaining to food. These made sense in ancient times when there was no refrigeration and people knew little about how disease was spread. But, they knew it had to do with how food was prepared sometimes. In some religions there is even a rule designating which hand a person shall use to perform personal cleansing.

"Hundreds of religious rules, or as you say, 'Thou shalt nots' came into being for reasons of health, economics, business—the list is endless; but the ones that govern society in general, mostly have to do with individual righteousness. Take the Ten Commandments. Whether you believe God personally wrote these down, or that Moses and the elders believed they were necessary to maintain tribal harmony, they still remain laws that are essential to a good and orderly society. For example: You are commanded not to covet. Now coveting doesn't sound like something illegal, fattening or immoral, does it? Well, think about it. If some individuals with little resistance covet something long enough, they are liable to turn to big crime like theft or robbery. As for adultery, that's simple. It could and still can get you killed.

"There were and still are good and logical reasons for the rules that evolved from religion, many of which have become civil laws in some nations. Thinkers in the church, countless theologians and even Plato have generally held that the laws and ideas that direct man's soul, or spirit, toward a higher plain—goodness—are the laws of God himself. Obedience to these rules seems to contribute to individual happiness, or a healthy outlook on the world. Disobedience, on the other hand, has brought man misery and tears. Plato knew there were skeptics, especially when it came to a system of punishments and rewards, such as heaven and hell, and he struggled at one point to find a natural ethic that would stir men to righteousness. He didn't find it and people aren't finding it today.

"Lance, all I can say is that if you break the rules of the church you generally end up getting hurt and often times hurting others. Hey, we've plunged into a pretty hefty topic."

"If I thought I could," said Lance, "I'd try, really try to follow all the rules. It would make me a stronger person; but I know as well as I am sitting here that it wouldn't last, that I'd eventually slide back and break whatever rule it was." He fumbled for his cigarettes, offered one to Martine, and after lighting it let the smoke curl gently upward from his nostrils. "Don't smoke?" I see.

"I do, but I'm trying to quit for the hundredth time," said Martine noticing that Lance was beginning to show his drinks.

"I have a feeling about you, Martine," said Lance heavily. "Quitting anything is no problem for you. You're one of those fortunate people born with natural resistance and self-control. You can resist anything that comes your way, if you really want to. You don't even have to pray about it, do you? Now, tell me, is that fair for the rest of us? You have all this stored-up resistance to doing wrong—like an inoculation against sin—so it's no sweat for you to tell the rest of us that we can follow the rules just by deciding that's what we are going to do. Come on, Martine, you've got to be kidding. It's not that easy for the rest of us weak mortals. Have a little pity."

The smile on Lance's face was soft. "You can't hide it, Martine.

There is a something inside you—it's like a little transmitter. It radiates goodness, and I feel it just the way other people do and am attracted to it. In some strange way I want to be a part of that goodness through a lasting friendship with you, the kind of friendship that Plato wrote about." Lance placed his palm momentarily on top of Martine's folded hands resting on the table.

Martine was embarrassed, feeling that the eyes of every patron in the lounge were trained on their table. Not wanting to offend Lance, yet desperate to escape Martine deftly turned the motion into a handshake. He wondered fleetingly what it was about the Camerons that gave them such power to embarrass him.

Lance sensed Martine's discomfort and explained, "You'll have to forgive me, Padre, but when I drink I sometimes get a little too affectionate; and I know that isn't done, even in the church world where you are supposed to love everybody!"

"Lance, you can be a part of the goodness we both create around us by being friends," said Martine regaining his composure, "but friendship must not be a selfish thing aimed at our own pleasure and security. I expect, in fact require, that we use it to contribute something of value to the lives of others—make their existence better and brighter; but we'll talk of that later.

"For now, Lance, I want to make sure you have a clear picture of what it is you expect of me and what I can give you both as a person and as a priest. If I have any of the virtue that you perceive as goodness then it is not something that can be transferred from me to you like a transfusion. Each person, and that includes you, must build their own treasury of good through their good deeds, thoughts and intentions. You can't borrow goodness from me. It doesn't work that way. I can help you work toward your own good life, and that's pretty much all that any caring person can do for another human being.

"Holy Moses, look at the time, and besides, I'm lecturing. Bad habit of mine. Lance, I must go. That six o'clock Mass comes earlier than you think."

Out in the brisk night air, Lance's head seemed to clear and he drove without incident the few miles to Martine's studio in Pueblo San Carlo. Martine thanked his host warmly for the sparkling evening.

"It's going to be a great summer, Padre," said Lance. "It's going to be great with the two of us. Don't forget our pact; and honestly, Padre, I love you for what you are. Adios!"

The Jeep tore away, lifting a shower of gravel as Martine looked after the departing young Cameron. Everything around him was dark and secret, seemingly drugged into slumber by the smoke from the ubiquitous burning piñon wood. From where he stood he could see stars still shimmering over the brooding Sangre de Cristo Mountains.

Once inside his warm apartment, Martine looked in the mirror and said to himself out loud, "What a strange evening." He didn't go to the church for his evening offices, but rather went through them hurriedly in his bedroom, skipped his shower and literally jumped into his bed. Sleep was slow in coming as his mind stayed awake examining these unusual past hours.

Martine was not given to any degree of suspicion about other people's actions because he tended to expect good, if not the best motives of everyone he met. However, he was surprised by the somewhat lavish warmth exhibited by Lance Cameron. On reconsideration, Martine remembered that he often drew this reaction from people, both men and women, and even from strangers. He suddenly remembered that in a New York subway once a little old lady had smiled at him and for no apparent reason took his hand fleetingly, saying before vanishing into the crowd, "Forgive me, young man, I just couldn't resist doing that."

Lance, though, was perplexing. He wondered what motivated the young man's premature professions of friendship. They really had little in common other than their youth, Martine thought. Perhaps Lance had grown up a lonely child in the isolation of his family's ranch, or maybe he was just one of those effusive individuals who cement all meetings, however brief, with a declaration of eternal friendship that then is promptly forgotten.

On second consideration, Martine wondered, could they be the kind of friends Lance almost seemed to insist they be? Martine was not sure that he needed intimate acquaintences who might complicate his work in the church at this delicate, incipient moment. Also, what might such a person demand of him that he would be unable to reciprocate. And, lastly, not at all unimportant: did he really like Lance Cameron.

THREE

San Luis Rey Church was rich in history. It was said that every governor of New Mexico since de Vargas, who reconquered the territory for the Spanish Crown in 1692 following the Indian revolt twelve years earlier, had worshipped in this ancient house of God. At the foot of the altar, carved in sandstone was the conqueror's name: Captain General Diego de Vargas Zapata Lujan Ponce de Leon y Contreras.

The church's collection of santos and other religious icons and statuary was one of the most extensive in the diocese. Martine never entered or left the church without taking note of them, almost as if they were special parishioners. Superior to all of them was the carving of David, supposedly a likeness of the Shepherd King when he was about Martine's age and bright with youth still free of the desires that corrupted him later. No one knew who carved this magnificent statue that depicted the sling that David used to slay the giant and the youth's rough garment of animal skin. Village legend held it was carved by the same woodworker who came mysteriously out of the desert to build without nails or pegs the spiral staircase for the nuns at the Chapel of Loretto in Santa Fe.

San Carlo women maintained the huge, two-towered church with its adobe walls twelve feet thick. These same women at least once each year, during the feast of one of the saints, renewed the walls, their hands working more adobe mud onto the exterior surfaces to eliminate cracks and peeling caused by inclement weather. This was how the walls had grown to citadel thickness over the centuries, keeping the church interior cool; through winter and summer the temperatures inside remained constant.

Martine liked the smell of the vanished years inside the church. He was there twice daily—in addition to morning Mass—to say his offices and spend time in meditation. Even without the small over-head electric candles, enough yellow daylight filtered into the church from small square windows twenty feet above the floor to outline pews and other furniture. And always there were banks of prayer candles burning at the sides of the altar, and a permanent votive light that illuminated the area where the Blessed Sacrament was reserved. He had just concluded his late afternoon prayers, blessing himself with the sign of the Cross, when someone opened one of the ponderous main doors to the church, admitting a light the color of old brass. A man's silhouette stepped into the slanting illumination but moved no further. He was searching for someone in the gloom, perhaps Martine.

"I'm here," Martine called out as he genuflected and walked briskly toward the door. His eyes, finally adjusted to the daylight.

"Lance!" said Martine with surprise. "What are you doing here at this hour?"

"Is there a special hour for the natives who come to the temple of the gods in supplication?" Lance asked, his smile brighter than the outside light.

Martine could see he had been drinking, and was still holding a beer in his hand.

"You know you can't do that in here," Martine said in exaspera-tion. "You can't bring beer into a church, Lance. Give it to me." Martine took the slightly tepid can, reached outside and set it down on one side of the step.

"Where is the welcome, the friendliness?" asked a seemingly contrite Lance, and then holding up one finger as if in admonish-ment, "Remember 'Be ye therefore kind unto strangers for whereby have some entertained angels unawares.' That's gospel, I forget just which one," and he turned to the nearest pew, knelt and whispered a brief litany. He arose, then took Martine by the elbow and led him outside.

"Hey friend, it's after five," declared Lance. "I've come to rescue you from ecclesiastical bondage and buy you a beer."

Martine was tired, a rare thing to intrude on his usually energetic pace; but the day had been a succession of meticulous tasks. Besides morning Mass and clearing his office of a portion of church paper-work, he had visited two parishioners, conducted a church class and officiated at a native burial service.

Perhaps a beer would be relaxing, just as it used to be following hours of stressful study at Cornell, and he was vaguely curious about judging what beneficial affect, if any, his last conversation might have had on Lance

"Okay," said Martine with enthusiasm, then quickly changed. "Oh, no, I can't. I promised Dalrymple I would drop a book by his place after five today."

"Okay," replied Lance. "We'll go by your place and get the book. I'm pretty certain there's room for it in the Jeep, and we'll go by Old Dal's place first. I know where he lives. Anyway, you'll probably want to leave that collar at home because I don't have enough money on me to buy for it, too.

They laughed comfortably as Martine closed the massive church door. He picked up Lance's beer from the step and took a long drink from the warm contents as they walked toward the Jeep. They drove the few paces to his studio.

∎

Dalrymple was on one of his favorite topics: the desecration of Santa Fe by hucksters, carpetbaggers and other exploiters.

"Father Martine doesn't understand this yet," the artist was saying, "but Santa Fe, the nation's oldest capital, a city that once was the mecca of great painters, writers and artists who were known worldwide for their creativity and talent, is being—has been—Californicated, all in the name of a buck. It's being sold lot by lot, block by block to people with big dollars who think the city is quaint and artsy and somehow this is going to rub off on them, when in reality they know as much about art as my cat over there." He motioned to a huge, yellow feline sleeping near the fireplace.

"What is Californicated?" asked Martine. "Sounds like some kind of deadly sin."

"That means it's being screwed just like California was," said Dalrymple. "In other words, our city's beauty, Old World charm and color are being exploited for money; and the people with the big bucks, the beautiful people from Hollywood who want Santa Fe for background to make them look a little more glamorous, are buying up the city as if it were some kind of commodity to be traded on the market. Good god, these so-called beautiful people are buying our city out from under us and they have no taste and no standards. With their kind of money they have inflated the price of everything. A simple little, two-bedroom adobe, built by some Mexican for maybe a couple of thousand bucks a few years ago, is selling now for half a million.

"This means that poor working folks, your waiters and cooks and clerks—all your service people—can't afford to live in their own city anymore. They have to live out of Santa Fe in a trailer or in another town and spend money driving long distances to work here every day. It's obscene."

Dalrymple had been painting again. His latest, "The Deposition," was an extremely large religious work showing the removal of the dead Christ's body from the cross following the crucifixion. The principal figures, the grieving Blessed Mother, Jesus' sorrowful brothers and a stricken Mary Magdalene, were depicted boldly and resembled American country people. Style-wise, Dalrymple identified with the midwestern painter, Thomas Hart Benton.

"Look at our downtown," the artist said as he scraped at a palate covered with years of dried paint. "It's not a downtown anymore. It's a vast mercenary flea market dealing in tourist gewgaws. Between the beautiful people and the tourists it's a doomed city. I expect any day to see in front of the cathedral a sign that says: 'See priest at altar—only $1.' And give them time, they will remove the Indian vendors and their jewelry from the Palace of the Governors and replace them with Hollywood actors trained as Indians, selling jewelry made in Taiwan. Then Californication will be complete."

He put down his palate and brushes, wiped his hands on his paint-stained apron and opened three more beers. Leaning back in a chair covered with a Navajo blanket, he lit a cigarette, an indication that he had rather talk than work. The smoke mingled with the odors of paints, lacquers and varnish.

"So, Lance, you're home from the books for the summer?" said Dalrymple. "What are you studying at the university? What's your major?"

"I've changed majors a couple of times," Lance replied. "I started out in business and darn near died of boredom. I'm concentrating on English lit right now. I have to make a decision this fall; but, Dal, getting back to this deterioration of Santa Fe. What do you think can be done about it, if anything?"

"It may be too late," said Dalrymple briskly. "I think the first thing we have to do is realize this city is first the home of a lot of people, and not some kind of carnival sideshow for tourists to gawk at. Once that is firmly in the minds of the city council and the chamber of commerce and all the other hucksters then maybe we can put a damper on the madness for more and more growth. Growth just means more people coming in, demanding more and more services that cost more and more money. This drive for growth is one of the reasons our city is selling its soul. A no-growth policy would be a start, coupled with some type of cap put on the price of real estate. Oh, yeah, I know it would draw howls from all the special interests, but fellows, we're talking about the loss of our city as we've always known it. A lot of its special flavor and spirit have already been lost. And you can chalk it all up to greed."

"Maybe, as Wordsworth once phrased it," said Martine, "you're looking before and after and wishing for what is not? You can't go back to what you remember Santa Fe was like when you were growing up here; and certainly you can't stop growth—progress."

"You can do anything you have the resolve to do," said Dalrymple. "Look at the places on the West Coast and how their city councils have adopted no-growth plans, and they are working, too. They just tell visitors and everybody else, come visit us, spend your money, but don't stay.

"Martine, can you imagine what this city used to be like before the carpetbaggers got a hold of it? It was a center for the arts, religion and government. Our business here was culture. That's what people worked at and it was a good life. We need a great leader to come forth again like Archbishop Jean Lamy. Do you know that he not only reorganized the church, which was disintegrating and on its last leg in the territory and built the cathedral, but he founded the first public schools and was even instrumental in bringing the Santa Fe Railroad here. Now there was a leader."

"Sounds to me like he was into the growth business," said Martine.

"It was a different kind of growth at a time when this was pretty much raw frontier," said Dalrumple impatiently. "And he was a different kind of leader. He had heart as well as soul. He wasn't in it for himself."

Dalrymple leaned far back in his big chair so that his jet black ponytail hung down behind his head as he rested it just at the top of the chair back. He lit another cigarette as he continued, "This is a story you especially need to hear, Martine." Oh, boy, thought Martine, he's really started now and we'll be here 'til midnight.

"Lamy came out here from France with nothing but his trunk, but he had this belief that if you treat people fair and keep them informed they will do amazing things for themselves and for you, too, comes the time when you have to ask their help. This meant having a lot of heart and treating people all the same. That's why he thought nothing of bringing French priests out to the diocese that was essentially Spanish in culture. It worked after a while because he treated everyone with the same fairness: Mexicans, French, protestants, Jews, you name it.

"Although you, Martine, haven't been here very long, you've seen La Conquistadora, probably the most revered sacred icon to Catholics in the Western Hemisphere, enshrined in her special chapel in the cathedral. She came here with some of the first Spaniards in 1625 as Our Lady of the Assumption; and she was one of the few things taken with them when they fled the native rebellion in 1680. However, when the reconquest of the territory was underway in 1693, the rebellious pueblo leaders at Santa Fe fielded an army that out-numbered the Spaniards; but the native resistance was quickly broken anyway, and the Spaniards attributed their victory to Our Lady of the Assumption who was in their ranks and returning to Santa Fe. That's why she was rechristened La Conquistadora.

"On high holy days Archbishop Lamy would lead Santa Fe's Catholics in solemn processional through the city, carrying La Conquisadora under the holy baldachin on their shoulders. On one such occasion, it was extremely hot and the archbishop suggested they pause midway through the ceremonial, place La Conquistadora and her trappings under a shade tree while the people entered a nearby saloon to get water for their thirst. When they returned to continue the procession, as you've probably guessed, La Conquistadora had vanished. The people were desolate and the archbishop was beside himself but to no avail; the holy icon was nowhere to be found.

"A prominent Santa Fe resident at that time was Jacob Spiegelberg, a Jewish merchant who had one of the city's very excellent and flourishing businesses. When his wife was putting their small daughter to bed on the evening of the icon's disappearance, she discovered to her horror that there was a large beautifully gowned doll on the pillow beside the child. The mother did not need to be told what had happened. It was all quite clear, but how could she tell the archbishop and how would he react? She telephoned him in tears and he came over immediately to retrieve the wandering La Conquistadora. He told Mrs. Spiegelberg to dismiss the incident from her thoughts because it came about under perfectly normal circumstances that anyone could understand.

"Later that year, Lamy had to go back to France and while he was away visiting, a large package arrived at the Spiegelbergs' home, addressed to the little girl. It was a doll—almost an exact duplicate of La Conquistadora. It was from the man who had heart and understood the human condition. That's what we need again today."

"That's a great story, Dal," said Martine. "I would liked to have known the archbishop. You can still feel his influence in the city today, and I don't mean just his statue standing in front of the cathedral."

"Now that we've drunk up all your beer," said Lance, "we need to be going. Why don't you come with us, Dal, and we'll have a couple at Los Dos Tortugas?"

"Not tonight," replied the artist. "I still need to get a little more work in."

∎

"Look, the cowboys have arrived," Poncho, the bartender, shouted across the room when he saw Lance and Martine enter and head for a booth.

"And my men are tying their horses outside," said Lance with a laugh, "so the service had better be top notch. We want the works: whiskey, women, cards. Bring it all." Turning to Martine, he said, "I've been coming here since I was in high school."

Atmosphere was one of the main offerings of this venerable Santa Fe lounge located not far from where the Old Santa Fe Trail once ended. It was here that businessmen of every hue, drummers (as peddlers were known a century ago), politicians, gamblers and ladies of the night gathered when the stage came in from Las Vegas,

New Mexico, to the east. The old watering hole was still something of Santa Fe in microcosm, attracting ranching people, Hispanics, a smattering of artists and a few politicians who could figure on panhandling a few more free drinks here than at the La Fonda.

Martine was still adjusting to the surroundings when Lance said, "You know, asking for cards isn't as absurd as it sounds. That's just what they used to do here. In fact, my dad rememebers when there was gambling everywhere in the state, but I guess the Baptists in the Legislature finally ran it all off to Nevada. Now only us Catholics and the Indians have what's left of it in the form of our bingo games and the casinos. You don't think gambling is immoral, do you?"

"It's not a question of morality," replied Martine. "It's a question of life style. If you only have a little money and gamble it away, leaving your family to go hungry, then I would say that's immoral. On the other hand, if you have lots of money and it amuses you to lose it at the gaming tables, then have at it. That helps spread the wealth and benefits the church or the Indians or whoever."

There was a pause as the waitress brought the beers, and Martine wondered where Lance might lead the conversation in his obvious attempt to draw him out. He admitted to himself that he was more drawn to Lance now than he had been at first. Perhaps they really were becoming friends, after all, but he wondered how the great difference between them could be reconciled. The church was his life and the power of God was real and tangible, while Lance, if not indifferent to the church, certainly treated it as a routine to be followed like checking tires and fuel level once a week.

What did he see in Lance, precisely? He had turned this over in his mind a number of times, always coming up with nothing he could put his finger on. Lance was free of constraints and pursued a devil-may-care life. Perhaps, Martine thought, he was drawn to this quality because he, while very free, accepted the rules and con-straints of the church as disciplines within which one worked and accomplished goals. Was Lance becoming an irrestible challenge that was luring him, holding out the tantalizing promise that he could tame this wild spirit and channel it into the service of God and man? He wondered how far he could be led into the boy's alien world before crying out, "enough!" He looked at the handsome face and laughing eyes under their crown of wild, blond hair and tried to fathom the nature of the being that inhabited such a magnificent temple.

"What are you looking at, what do you see?" Lance asked with curiosity. "I know what you were doing. You were looking into my soul and estimating what kind of remodeling work was needed there and how you might go about it."

"Does it need remodeling? You have a guilty conscience?"

"There's no guilt," said Lance. "I'm a very happy person. I have everything I need. I sense that you, too, are a very happy person, Martine. You look...what's the word...serene. That's it. I started to say angelic, but that's pretty corny, probably even offensive by today's standards and meanings. Yes, you are happy, but there is some sort of armor about you."

"It wards off evil," said Martine with a slight smile. "It can't be penetrated by the bad guys."

"Quick, give me a definition of evil as you understand it," Lance ordered.

"Something against God; something against man," replied Martine. "Disobedience is evil, hating people is evil, even neglect of people is evil, hurting people is evil, destroying the good works of God and man is evil, greed is evil."

"I may disobey a little," said Lance, "but I don't think I'm into those other things. I might just be in pretty good shape. Hey, you'll really like me when you get to know me."

"But to what use are you putting those things that have been given you?" asked Martine. "You've been given health, talent, ability, looks and intelligence. Giving something back is why man is here and through giving he grows, demonstrating to everyone how inter-dependent we are on one another. We are here to serve, Lance."

"Gee whiz, Padre. I knew you would put a stinger in there somewhere. I don't have time to serve. I'm too busy preparing myself so I can do some of the things you are talking about. But, then, again, there are just a whole heck of a bunch of people who don't deserve anything more than what they have. It's usually their fault if they are poor and hungry. They ought to get out and work for it."

"Are we to judge who is worthy?" asked Martine. "Shouldn't each of us be concerned about whether we are worthy? And we should be setting the example and serving without regard to who is worthy. Man's only salvation, for himself and for the world, is in giving of himself. Just lay aside religious precepts for a moment and think about our world. If we don't start sacrificing for its improvement and for the good of others, I seriously doubt it can be saved.

"If people could only understand that by serving and saving the world, they serve and save it for themselves. Instead most people today—especially in our country—are dedicated to the belief that we can have it all: peace on earth, high tech, great family life. Most people are in the world now to take these things, not to give. In fact, more and more our society is structured so individuals cannot practice charity directly, one on one. If they give at all, it is through agencies where they don't have to see the plight of the needy. We have been insulated from them and thus if they are out of sight, they are out of mind.

"And so many people also destroy what God has provided. They rape the land of its trees and vegetation, completely indifferent to the fact that as earth's covering goes it takes with it the very air we breathe and the atmosphere that protects us from the sun. They've made an industry out of the slaughter of the earth's creatures, large and small, just to rip from their dead bodies trinkets and trophies for the market.

"If you still don't believe in the power of evil and its presence in this world, then consider the unparalleled rapaciousness, cruelty and death that man in the twentieth century has inflicted on his own kind, with no regard for the innocent. Attempts at exterminating whole peoples because of their nationality, religion or class have nearly succeeded; and people have suffered and died by the tens of millions at the hands of others in Russia, Germany, Turkey, China, Cambodia and in a dozen nations in Africa. We will not escape judgment. But here I am again, sermonizing."

"Speaking of no escape—I believe we are about to be snared by one Cindi Salazar," said Lance as he nodded toward a vivacious young woman moving in their direction."

"She's very pretty," observed Martine.

"!Hola! ¿Que Pasa, Lancito?" said Cindi, moving the flat of her hand in a high, swinging arch. "Whenever have I seen two more gorgeous hunks together in one place?"

"Cindi, I want you to meet Martine dePaul," said Lance. "Martine, this is Cindi Salazar; and Cindi, let me warn you before you start twirling your lasso, he's already taken. Married. He's a wax apple."

Martine winced at Lance's use of the word married, although he was married in a way, but he knew Cindi had taken Lance's words for their traditional meaning.

"When did being married ever stop one of you men from getting what you wanted?" asked Cindi as she sat down tightly against Lance without letting him move over. She ran her fingers sensuously through his hair as her lips pursed closely to his face. "Besides, this is what I want some of—not to hurt your feelings, Martine. Perhaps another time when you don't feel quite so married. But Lance and I have been lovers since forever. You live in Santa Fe, Martine? Why haven't I seen you around before?"

"No," stammered Martine. "I don't live here. I just visit in the city." He was aware how her body language and Lance's had become unabashedly sexual. Cindi's hand was now inside Lance's loose shirt, languidly massaging his powerful and pronounced back muscles. Lance's arm enveloped her waist and his hand vanishing somewhere into the folds of her blouse.

"Cindi and I met in high school," said Lance. "She was a year or two ahead of me, but she was the Circe I couldn't quite resist, nor could any other guy if she gave him half a chance. Of course, you know what happened to the men who let Circe lure them away?"

"They were turned into swine," said Martine. "So that's your excuse, Lance?"

They all laughed as Lance replied: "I was always able to resist Cindi's sorcery just enough. All the other guys couldn't and wound up in the pig lot."

"You didn't resist anything, Muchacho," said Cindi, pouting. "You forget the time my Papa caught us on the sofa...."

"Cindi!" Lance interrupted, "Don't reveal all the sordid details to Martine. We need to hold back a few secrets to keep an aura of fascination for him." His lips, moistened and gleaming, touched her ear lightly.

"Martine, if you'll excuse us for a little while," said Lance, "we are going to dance and then I'll run Cindi home. She needs a ride. I'll be back in half an hour or so. You won't be...you don't mind, do you? You'll stay 'til I get back? I'll order another beer as I pass the bar."

"Where would I go without wheels?" Martine said quietly as Lance and Cindi whirled out onto the dance floor to a lively Mexican tune. She blew a kiss back over Lance's shoulder, her dark eyes blazed a smile and then they were gone.

Something was very wrong with such a frank and open sexual display, Martine thought; but why was he not resentful? The atmosphere had been electric with their lust, their glances. Their touching and rapid breathing had been blatant, seminal signs of the act they anticipated and doubtless were engaging in at this very moment, he thought.

Martine wondered if Lance could have staged this bizarre performance to see how he would react. Did he hope to corrupt a man of God by seeing him become aroused in some vicarious participation. But no one would engage in such a sick experiment on another, all just to satisfy a perverted curiosity. Strangely he was not outraged, not even angry. In fact, he suddenly realized he was fighting a tinge of envy, almost a desire to be like Lance. He shook himself out of this fantasy, blaming these strange, confused feelings on too much alcohol. His mouth was dry and he ordered another beer while he waited.

The promised half-hour became more than twice that and Martine's one beer was followed by two more before Lance finally returned, disheveled and desolate over being away from his guest for so long.

"So, you finally returned," said Martine grimly. "I thought you were gone for the evening."

"Aw, come on Martine. You know I wouldn't leave you stranded. Sorry it was so long, but you wouldn't believe what all I had to do."

"Oh, but I would believe—very much believe," said Martine knowingly. "I only have one thing to say. I am astonished that you choose to sin so openly before the church, having your parish priest as virtually a member of the audience to your concupiscence."

Lance's face became a mask of grief as he lay back length-wise in the booth, draping his boots out over the arm rest and taking a deep drink from his beer. "Martine, there's no way I would injure your feelings deliberately; and I can see that what Cindi and I did was very inconsiderate, very insensitive. The only excuse I can offer is that when she gets near me, I just lose control. Martine, when I feel that rise in my groin, I can't help myself. It takes over and it rules me. But I'm only making it worse by confessing my inmost feelings and desires to you. I just can't keep from hurting your feelings."

Again, the envy appeared far in the recesses of Martin's mind.

He repressed it before he spoke. "Look, Lance, I'm your confessor. It's my duty to hear your buried thoughts, hidden desires, things that you can share with no one else; however, my role is not as an accomplice or to be treated to graphic descriptions of your anatomy's reaction to sexual stimulus. I cannot sit still for that or anything remotely like it and then turn around and ask absolution for your sins against God. And, by the way, you don't hurt my feelings. You just disappoint me."

"Perhaps I was needlessly indelicate, Martine; but the world is an indelicate place, and I only wanted you to get a sense of the coarseness of ordinary people like myself, people who can never be in a state of grace no matter how much or how hard they try. And I don't think all the absolution in the world is going to help me get control of this aspect of my life. My sex drive has always had control of my judgment, and Martine, if it's that powerful and I was born with it, I sometimes can't see how I am commiting a sin by putting to good use what God gave me, especially when it feels so great and is also so great for my partner."

"Lance, the point I've been trying to get over to you since we first met is that we can conquer self and in so doing, we can conquer the world. Henry Ward Beecher said there is no liberty for men whose passions are stronger than their religious feelings; and that there is no liberty for men who know not how to govern themselves. This concept is at the very root of individual faith."

Martine downed the beer "Look, it's way after midnight and morning Mass comes awfully early. We can't resolve this here to-night; but, Lance, you are making a start by analyzing the nature of your struggle, and in time to come we will pursue this thing until we both find the right answers."

▮

Sixty feet below them on the trail, their horses were loosely tethered so the two animals could nibble while Lance and Martine sat on the crown of Squaw Rock looking out over the Rio Grande Valley. From this point they could see far below them the Three-J Ranch sprawling away from the Sangre de Cristo Mountains; and on the distant side of the valley was the wall of the blue Jemez Mountains bearing like a nest in its arms the city of Los Alamos and its vast laboratories out of which came the bomb that intimidated two generations of mankind and changed the world forever. Lance, physically fit from his work on the ranch, had scaled the steep sandstone rock formation first and sat at the top smoking as he chided Martine about his snail's pace progress up the rock face that early settlers had named Squaw because they thought it resembled an Indian woman.

Martine had not wanted to make the climb, or even come on this outing to Cameron Ranch, but had been pressured into it by Amanda Cameron. She and Lance's sister Rebecca had caught Martine off guard as they left the church from early morning Mass and would listen to none of his pleas about his work load. They had insisted that he spend the day at the ranch relaxing with food, drink and a hiking trip Lance had planned.

"Father Martine," Amanda had announced in an ebullient voice outside the church, "that boy absolutely adores you. I don't know when I've seen him so impressed with anyone. Why, he's quoting you on one subject or another with every breath he draws, and I can already detect a change in him. I attribute this directly to your influence this summer. Oh, I so hope he will follow your example and enter the priesthood."

A wry smile crossed Martine's face as he thought of Lance in a priestly setting along with his baser pursuits. He had gotten to know a great deal about this young rancher over the past month or so because Lance had devised endless ways in which the two of them were thrown together one way or another. He would often attend the early Mass then stay on for breakfast, or he and Dalrymple would perch on the young priest's doorstep until Martine would accompany them to discover the latest artistic creation just unveiled in one of Santa Fe's many galleries. There were countless other ploys: invitations to dinner, dropping by with a few beers or word of a new band at Los Dos Tortugas. Lance never seemed to run out of things to celebrate, ranging from his sister's birthday to the anniversary of the purchase of his favorite riding horse. But there seemed to be nothing special behind this latest invitation to the ranch. It had appeared to be Amanda's idea until Martine heard her shout from the Three-J Jeep before she drove away from the church: "Now, come straight on out, Father Martine. Lance would be so disappointed if you didn't."

"So, Martine, what do you think of the old Three-J now that you can see it from overhead like an eagle?" asked Lance.

"It's larger than some small countries," said Martine. "I can think of several that are smaller than your ranch: San Marino, Monaco, Liechtenstein, Mauru—there must be a dozen others."

"Hey, you forgot the most important one of all," said Lance. "Vatican City! Wait until the Pope hears about this."

"Well, yeah, but it's more like a principality or city state. I never think of it as a country so much as the home office of the church."

"How about Andorra?" asked Lance with an eager smile.

"No, not really. It's larger and takes up a good chunk of the Pyrenees Mountains between France and Spain."

"Have you been there, too?"

"Yes, once when I was a teenager and traveling with my folks. It's a beautiful place, kinda like the country setting for one of those nineteenth century operettas."

"It must be something to grow up like that," said Lance with a note of awe in his voice. "You were not only able to get your education any place you chose, but you could travel to the most exotic places imaginable and learn first hand about countries and people that most of us will only ever read about."

"Oh, I don't know," said Martine. "It wasn't always as glamorous and exciting as you might imagine."

"Did you have friends and girls and all the normal things that average kids have?"

"Of course I did," said Martine with an edge of exasperation to his voice.

"Well, hey, you know everything about me," said Lance, "so I think it's only fair I know something about you. Now, don't get sore, but did you ever get any?"

The question did not affect Martine, but there was a long pause before he answered: "I think I always believed, even as a kid and a teenager, that God was watching me, taking note of everything I did. I didn't believe that sex then—outside of marriage—was acceptable to Him. It was unacceptable to the church under those circumstances, and Lance, it still is."

"Gosh, I'm sorry I asked," said Lance, withdrawing into himself, making a gesture with his head and shoulders that imitated a turtle.

"No, no, don't get me wrong. I wasn't irked at your question. I was just trying to give you a credible answer in this cynical age that pretty much doesn't accept answers based on personal morality."

"So, what do you think of this age? How do you personally assess it?"

"It's an ugly age that's lost its soul," said Martine with sadness. "People have rejected the rules and standards men once lived by for a hedonist philosophy of total immersion in materialism and lust. They have rejected the world of the mind and the spirit for self-indulgence, and they have abandoned charity for lives of acquisition and avaraice. And if there are no longer any rules, or guides, or sign posts to point the way for man, and if he no longer believes in the commands of God, what is to follow but a world of anarchy in which every ineffable crime and unspeakable act will become common place. Civilization will vanish and what remains of the community of man will become an environment of hell. What can I think of such a vision of horror?"

"But Padre," said Lance wide-eyed and with a voice filled with gravity, "aren't you being a bit melodramatic? Is the world really becoming that bad?"

"There are signs of the deterioration and inevitable collapse all around you. It's in our vile language in public, in the way we dress ourselves, in our loss of manners, civility and respect toward other people, in our indifference to the suffering and tragedy that strike whole nations of people. Consider our entertainment programs in which the most offensive language imaginable is used before millions of people. This is condoned by calling it entertainment, but don't forget that it is also being marketed by the greedy for the great deluge of dollars it generates."

"Wow, you really know how to lay it on them," said Lance. "So, what can we do?"

"I don't know that you can do anything to stop the collapse of this burned-out age," said Martine. "The individual can still strive for those achievements of the mind and spirit that make human life better, but I wouldn't bet on the success of a worldwide spiritual reformation even if all of us started working on it now. It may be irreversible, inevitable."

"Head for the hills," said Lance in mock alarm. "Look at those hills and coves, Martine. They are filling up with darkness. We've talked the sun down from the sky. Let's head back before it gets too dark to find our way home."

∎

San Estevan of Acoma stands taller than any church in America. Its foundation of solid stone plunges three hundred eighty feet to the flat desert floor. The bell towers on the nearly three-hundred-year-old church rise upward seventy feet to bear simple white wooden crosses. The foundation is the great mesa rock that pushes this "Sky City" toward the clouds. The city has been home to the Acoma people for at least one thousand years.

The rock was also fortress and impregnable bastion for the Acomas, who were once the most warlike and independent of the Southwest's native people. Their city of stacked adobe apartments atop the imposing mountain of stone was initially inaccessible to the marching armies of the Spanish conquest. There was no road, or trail or path to the sky. Only handholds and indentations in the sheer rock face led to the top and these were the secret of the skilled Acoma climbers.

In the sixteenth century, from the rock ramparts, a handful of Acoma warriors wielding bows and arrows and spears were able, at first, to hold off the Spanish army that had subdued the rest of the surrounding pueblos as subjects for the crown. The only equal to these defenses in the world was the Jewish fortress of Masada near the Dead Sea. From 72 to 73 A.D. that towering fortress stone defied the Roman legions. The seige ended only with the defenders' suicide. Eventual subjugation of the Acomas also ended in apocalypse.

"How did the Spaniards finally manage to scale those walls?" asked Martine.

"I don't know," replied Lance. "I don't think I've ever seen this explained in any story concerning the defeat of the Acomas by Don Juan de Oñate's army."

The two were sitting in Acoma rock's shadow eating ears of roasted corn they had bought from a village woman after they visited San Estevan Church. Like all visitors, they had walked to the top and later descended on the narrow rock ledge that was chopped out in later years to provide access by foot.

Martine, having read Willa Cather's "Death Comes for the Archbishop" in college, had known about Acoma and its church for a number of years, but he did not particularly want to make the one hundred-mile trip to the shrine when Lance brought the matter up. "Hey, guy, it's the Fourth of July and you don't have another thing planned," he told Martine over the phone.

"If you've never seen it, I'll guarantee it's breath taking." Martine finally gave in and went along reluctantly.

But, it was everything Lance had promised. When Martine first glimpsed the city towering above the flat desert floor he was still three miles away on the canyon rim rock. "It's really an enchanted place. It makes me think of Babylon's hanging gardens," he told Lance who smiled with satisfaction because at last he had impressed the sophisticated and knowledgeable priest. It was cool now as the desert shadows lengthened and they sat pondering the massive stone that in one way had changed the history of the American Southwest.

"After a number of attempts, the Spanish soldiers sent out by Oñate finally did scale these walls," said Lance. "If I remember the story correctly it was on a cold January day in 1599 that ruin was visited on the proud Acomas. A troop under Vincente de Zaldivar slaughtered the city's inhabitants and then put the torch to their homes. Those Acomas that were captured were linked together with ropes and led away to stand trial under Govenor Oñate in the territorial capital, and you can imagine how fair a trial he conducted against a group of people who were considered heathen and savage. Besides, all the rest of the Indian tribes in the territory were on the verge of revolt and watching to see what punishment would be handed out to the rebellious Acomas.

"All male Acomas more than twenty-five years old were sentenced to have one foot chopped off and also to twenty years of slavery, while those between ages twelve and twenty-five were sentenced only to the twenty years of slavery. All women more than twelve years old received the same twenty-year sentence except for sixty young girls who were transported to convent servitude in Mexico City from which they would never return. Two Hopi men captured in the pueblo had one hand severed so they might bear living evidence of Acoma's destruction to other Indians in the territory. Cruel and inhumane as the Spaniards' retribution was, this example probably helped suppress any notions of revolt that other pueblo peoples in the territory might have had."

"You really know your history," said an impressed Martine.

"It was always a place that stirred my imagination—fascinated me," said Lance. "I used to like to think about how it could be fortified with modern weapons and hold off armies in modern times. Would you have wanted this as your church assignment?"

"It would have been fantastic," said Martine, "although you probably know the fate of one priest who was given this as his parish. The Acomas tossed him from one of the highest cliffs up there."

"Now that's one story I don't know," said Lance. "Is that in some church history?"

"No, it's in a story told by Willa Cather," said Martine. "The priest, one Father Balthazar I believe he was called, was made to pay for his sins against the Acoma people. He was a despot who finally carried his tyranny too far when he accidentally killed a serving boy in his household by throwing an object at him in a fit of temper. For years the monstrously fat priest had made virtual slaves of the Acomas. He made them carry soil in baskets to the top of the rock to create a garden with the best of fruits and vines. Then they were forced to carry water each day to save it from the blistering sun. He used the people as his servants, his cooks and his messengers and he appropriated from them the best of everything they produced or created. This went on for years until the boy's death.

"The Acoma men came in a group and bound Father Balthazar and took him to the cliff. After swinging him back and forth, they turned him loose and he fell to his death on the rocks below. With a record like that, Lance, I would think that future priests would watch themselves. And, I think we should put away our history books and head for home."

FOUR

Gusty winds swept rain in ghostly veils across San Carlo Pueblo. The towers of San Luis Rey Church glistened with rivulets as lightning flashes summoned them out of the darkness only to release them back into the black hole of night. Martine was part of this lightning-etched tableau as he stood in the church doorway watching the downpour and wondering if he should make a dash to his car and drive the short distance to his studio, or if the storm might offer a lull that would allow him to get home without being drenched. With brushes of dazzling fire, the lightning again and again displayed its artistry over the vast expanse of the Sangre de Cristo Mountains. They remained an ominous dark bulk, sodden under the onslaught.

Martine knew it was getting very late. He had come to the church after eleven o'clock to say his final offices before turning in. He had a vague idea of the time because he had looked at his watch before leaving Father Fabian Chavez' house where he had spent the evening. The old priest had declared the visit a special occasion and opened one of his rare wines, a bottle of Moulin au Vent 1937, and the two of them, buoyed by the richly textured drink, were so engrossed in conversation that they had not noticed the evening slipping away. Martine still felt a slight high from the wine. Aged vintage had this effect on him. Deep inside he had a twinge of doubt about engaging in things of the spirit when he had been drinking. On the other hand, it enhanced his spiritual feeling, giving him a sharper vision of his communication with God. Surely, if there was any fault to be found in the first thing, it was outweighed by the increase of virtue it brought about in the second.

The rain's tempo suddenly lessened. Martine took advantage of the break to slosh hurriedly to his car, not bothering to cover his head since his crew cut was easily restored with a rub or two from a towel. The Volkswagen engine turned over easily and he moved the vehicle slowly through the several inches of run-off water toward his studio. He almost didn't see the Jeep, parked off the road and at a crazy angle to the far corner of his studio. His headlights caught the vehicle's seal, the circled Js. A lightning flash fleetingly illuminated the Jeep's interior and revealed Lance Cameron slumped over the steering wheel. Martine's horn drew no response from the crumpled figure. Had Lance been in an accident, had he fallen asleep, or had he had too much to drink or possibly all three?

Martine jumped out of his car and in one bound was at the Jeep, jerking open the flimsy canvas door. Shaking the boy's limp shoulder, he shouted, "Lance! Lance, what's the matter? Are you all right?" The smell of alcohol indicated that he simply was very drunk and unable to drive and had gone to sleep while waiting for Martine to come home. He also was soaking wet from having been out in the rain. Vigorous shaking did nothing to awake him. Instead, he slipped slowly to the left side of the seat and had Martine not caught him in his arms, he would have fallen out of the Jeep.

There seemed to be only one solution. Martine would have to get the intoxicated youth into his studio. The rain had now grown heavier and thunder seemed to shake the buildings to their foundations. "Lance? Lance, come on now, we're going to get you inside," he said firmly.

The cold rain caused him to stir as Martine, with one arm around his waist, pulled him in a half-stagger toward the studio door. "Hey, man, wha's going on?" Lance said thickly. "Wha's happening? What'd I do?"

"It's okay," said Martine. "You're at my place. We're going to get you inside and get you dried off. With some hot coffee you're going to be all right. You've just had a few too many, that's all." When they reached the door, Martine used one hand to fumble with his key, while his other hand had the difficult task of keeping Lance propped against the wall. Inside, he eased the soaked youth into a chair by the fireplace and went to get a blanket.

"I'll light a fire and we'll get you warmed up," Martine assured his guest who was only faintly conscious. He draped the blanket around Lance, threw a dry towel over his head and turned to light the paper and wood in the fireplace. As the flames licked upward, he went to make coffee.

"It's a good thing I came home and found you there," he told Lance as he returned shortly with a cup of coffee and set it on the table in front of him. It steamed in the still cool room that the newly set fire had not had time to warm. "You could have caught pneumonia out there in those wet clothes."

Lance's eyes were open now as he groped at his shirt buttons, unfastening each one slowly as though not sure of how to manipulate them. He raised his head and looked at Martine with a partial smile. "Hey, man, where ya been? Been waitn' since two o'clock—I mean ten, an' m'ole buddy's not home."

"I was visiting Father Fabian," said Martine. "Come on, you're not making any progress with those wet clothes. I'll help you with the boots, and you take a drink of coffee. It'll warm you up."

He helped Lance pull off the soggy boots, old and badly scuffed, from riding and ranch work. As the fire warmed the room, Lance became more alert and with a single motion unsnapped his jeans, pulling them and his under shorts off together, out along his outstretched legs. He threw the wet garments toward the fireplace, then stood unsteadily and shucked off the wet shirt, letting it fall beside the chair with a sopping sound on the tiled floor. The fire light flickered over his tanned, sinewy body, and this brief moment of nudity seemed to surprise him. He hastily pulled the blanket Martine had brought around his chilled form. Martine quickly looked away.

As he sat down Lance shivered slightly. "Y'know whadded really warm me? I needa beer. Y'got some in the frige, don't ya? Yeah, an' y'need one, too," he said, rising and moving rockily toward the kitchen. Martine wondered what effect the beer, added to his wine, would have. He tried to think of the drinking formula he had learned at Cornell: beer on whiskey, awfully risky; wine on beer, never fear? No, that wasn't quite it. Anyway, the added beer, he thought, would reinforce his sleep.

Lance returned with the two beers. "Y'know," he said in a voice less impeded. "I wasn't really tapped out, out there. Out there in the Jeep, I mean. I jus' got sleepy waitn' for you, an' when I sleep I really go out." He noted the quizzical look on Martine's face. "Honestly," he said, "I wasn't all that smashed. I jus' got big sleepy. I'd been out last night, too, an' so I crashed. Really."

"Look," Martine said. "You don't have to explain. You're old enough to know what you're doing, however risky it may be. And if you get bombed sometimes, it doesn't mean you're any less masculine, any less a he-man, if that's what's bothering you."

"Hey, Padre, I don't care about the he-man stuff," said Lance. "I know I'm as masculine as the next guy. I jus' care what you think about me. I don't want you to think I'm some kind of lush." The very earth shook suddenly with a distant cannon-boom of thunder and lightning danced through the window's closed blinds. Rain was pounding heavier on the roof. "Here it comes again," said Lance. "I should have gone home while I had the chance."

Martine thought of the rough country road winding, sometimes tortuously, out to the Three-J ranch house and of the unbridged arroyos that crossed it. Sometimes, after heavy rains, he knew these so-called dips in the road could suddenly rush with torrents deeper than a car. Unsuspecting mortorists crossing what they believed were dry arroyos sometimes were caught and drowned by such unexpected floods. "Lance, it's out of the question. You're not going home in this storm. You're staying here until morning. We'll call Amanda. Your mother will be worried."

Lance drained his beer and went to get another while Martine telephoned the Cameron Ranch, waking Amanda. She thanked Martine and told him she was grateful that he had taken her son in out of the storm.

"I could sleep now," said Lance, yawning. "I hope your bed is comfortable, Martine."

"I'll get some covers and sack out here on the rug by the fire," Martine said.

"No way, man! If you're gonna do that, I'll just put my duds back on and drive myself out to the ranch. That bed is big enough for both of us...unless you have something that's catching," Lance said with a laugh.

"You're sure you don't mind?"

"No, why should I mind? It's your bed, and I'm not going to push you out of it."

"I just wanted to make sure you would be comfortable sleeping that way," said Martine. "Sometimes people are fussy about sleeping arrangements."

"Naw, not me," said Lance. "I can sleep anywhere anytime." He threw his cigarette butt in the fire and followed Martine to the bedroom. The thunder was more distant now but a loud rumble shook the bedroom window. "I hope that will stop," said Martine, "so it won't keep me awake."

"You should have had another beer," said Lance as he dropped his blanket and slid naked beneath the deep covers. He gave a hard shiver. "Oh, it's cold," he said.

Martine got in on the other side, reached out and clicked off the bedside lamp. The room was in semi-darkness, somewhat illuminated from the dying fire in the living room. He could feel the bed shake slightly. "Hey, Lance, are you going to be all right? You getting a cold or something?"

"I just need to get my temperature adjusted after leaving the fire."

"How about I put more cover over you?" asked Martine.

"No, not necessary," replied Lance, still shaking. "You know what would really help more than anything? Body heat. That's the way the Indians do it. Let me sleep next to you for a little. That will help to regulate my body's thermometer more than anything else."

Martine was embarrassed by the suggestion but could not find words to frame a reply that would not sound absurd. Before these thoughts were out of his mind, he could feel the warm, hard body of the young rancher against his shoulder and side.

Lance was still for a few moments and his chills subsided. "Wow, this feels great," he said, his voice muffled by the cover. "Thanks, Martine. It's just what I needed. I knew you wouldn't mind. What are friends for if they can't be close to one another?" He raised his head and looked at Martine's face.

Still the right words eluded Martine. His mouth was dry and he felt a flush run over him as somewhere that odd feeling of envy stirred in his mind again. "Glad you're warming up," he stammered slowly, still not knowing what to say, or how it should be said. He was glad to hear the rain growing louder on the roof, maybe smothering some of his awkwardness. Outside, the world was shaken by massive hands of thunder.

"Aw, it's so good," said Lance huskily, almost to himself. He shifted his body slightly and his powerful arm fell gently across Martine's chest. "It's fantastic having you as my best friend," he said sleepily.

Martine did not like feeling awkward. He was always self-assured because he was the one in command of situations involving other people. But with Lance he was not in command. He had no control of himself or any notion of how to take charge without making himself feel foolish. He wondered how this situation could be explained. It had to be happening because of Lance's drunkenness. This explanation came to him as he caught the strong alcoholic smell of Lance's warm breath near his face. He could quietly lift the youth's arm and just move to the far side of the bed and nothing more would be thought of the matter. Still, the feeling of having another human so close was dimly agreeable. Strangely, he was the one who now shivered.

"Hey, what's this, Old Buddy?" Lance's voice was a deep heavy whisper. "You're the one who's chilling now. You see I wasn't all that wrong about it being cold tonight. Just relax...we'll make it good. You'll feel better."

Lance's arm muscles slowly tightened against Martine's chest and his hand locked partially over his upper arm so he was being turned slowly to face Lance with the boy's body flat against his own. For some reason that had no logic, he could not resist this uninvited encroachment. Lance's other arm edged under his side into a complete embrace. Martine's chills were smothered by incredible warmth, his breathing was deep and heavy, nearly independent of his will.

"See, didn't I tell you—the chills are gone," said Lance in an almost profound whisper that was vibrant and directly in Martine's ear. The boy's head was lying against his own, and Martine's arms that before had been unyielding were now tightening around Lance's hard body. Strange physical sensations seemed to combine with that earlier feeling of envy into something Martine could recognize and identify with shock. It was desire gradually becoming passion, a desire to be enfolded into Lance's maleness.

"Oh, it's good, very good," said Lance in a whisper that was close to a moan of pleasure. Then, in a slightly apologetic tone, "I can't resist being affectionate to people I like, Martine. I just can't resist something I need so very much." His words were muffled, lost in his desire.

Martine still could find no words. Disbelief at what was happening had erased his voice. This was not something that had ever been part of his experience. He was shocked that the seed of such a desire had existed in his being all these years without his having the faintest awareness of it. It was like discovering a beautiful, fully furnished room that he had never known about because it had been cleverly sealed off. Among all the thoughts vying for his mind's consideration one was paramount: he had never really loved before in his life—had not loved with the flesh, with the senses, with raw sensuality. And even with all his youthful happiness, there had always been a void that he had never admitted to himself. Yes, he had been lonely, even when surrounded by friends and family. He wanted to shout "I'm not lonely for the first time in my life." Someone wanted him.

So overwhelming was this revelation, that his status as a priest of the Holy Catholic Church was shed like a chrysalis. In a moment's time he left his innocence behind him. All the moral teachings and defenses he had learned and believed in were abandoned, so over-whelming was the craving that possessed him. He could not reason with it. It offered no compromise. He felt exposed and defenseless in the path of an on-rushing force about which he knew nothing. It mesmerized him, closing out his old world without leaving a trace.

"What's wrong?" asked Lance in his deep, desirous whisper. "You haven't said a word. Isn't it good? Am I missing something, doing something wrong?"

Martine was so engrossed, yet so untutored in the ways of this strange, exotic realm he had entered for the first time that the only words he could mutter were: "It's incredible."

"Aw, Martine! Damn, how dumb of me," whispered Lance. "I should have known better. It's your first time and you're panicked. It's a blow to your whole system, to your values. Hey we've all had a first time. It's nothing to worry about. Millions of people do this. Just relax. Relax and enjoy it—let the feeling roll over you...let me show you."

Lance's large, well formed hands pressed flat palms against Martine's back. They were electric as they gently massaged his muscles and moved up Martine's body to his neck and hair where with great gentleness the fingers caressed his head. He was sur-prised at how tenderly the powerful young rancher communicated his emotions. In a mirror image, his own hands explored Lance's athletic splendor, touching and savoring the beauty of each muscle. Lance was pure sculpture, a work of chiseled beauty that rivaled Michelangelo's David.

"Ah, ah, ah," Lance cried out in throaty passion as he enveloped

Martine with his body and arms. Effortlessly he shifted his body weight so Martine was turned on his back with Lance's hungry frame covering him.

Martine responded by wrapping his arms around Lance, pulling him down closer so their chests were tightly together. It was an involuntary reaction, driven by undisciplined passion that blanked the mind and emotions to all but the amorous youth embracing him. Against his throat Lance's breath was tinged with fire. Martine surrendered himself entirely to the sheer physical power of the male body, its sexual aura, its heat, it's man aroma.

Lance's whispered, "You want me. You want all of me."

"Yes, yes, yes," was the only reply Martine could manage.

"Now, we fly away," Lance said fervently and his voice trailed off as his muscular body rippled into the familiar motion that he knew so well when he made love to women.

Dim, muffled sounds of thunder resembling the beat of the pueblo's drums on festival days broke over the Village of San Carlo and the rain was steady, but it was lost on Martine's ears now filled with the rush of Lance's breath and the rhythm of his vibrating body caught in the gentle fury of possession—a possession that enraptured both their bodies. The moments of heightening pleasure seemed an eternity to Martine, who felt he was being drawn out of himself by the body pulsating against his, yet in some inexplicable way he was possessing the very essence of Lance at the same time.

Lance's moans of gratification grew more powerful with his increasing momentum; and Martine, stimulated by the youth's sensuous, undulating muscles that controlled and manipulated his body, felt a growing pleasure within him that must soon burst taking with it his conscious being.

"Oh, Martine! Martine!" Lance cried as the pitch of his voice soared in pleasure. "This is it! Oh, yeah, yeah!" Lance was rendered helpless by the violent ecstasy that exploded within him. It also swept away the last barriers that had held back the swelling flood of wild rapture inside Martine and a raging tide plunged him into a deep vortex of ravishment. The intensity racked his body repeatedly with pure pleasure, finally releasing him both enervated and drained.

Lance eased over on his back, his nude body exhausted and gleaming with perspiration. "Martine," he said in a quiet, emotionless voice, "we are lovers. We have made love, finally. I never thought it would happen."

Martine could not reply as he listened to the distant sounds of the fading thunder. He wondered quietly if the life he had known and loved was fading also. His hand brushed against his cheek and he was astonished to find it wet from tears. Why were they there? What had prompted them?.

Lance slowly reached for his cigarettes and sat up in bed, smoking one in the dark. "What are you thinking?" he asked Martine. "Did this shock you? Do you find me contemptible now?"

There was a long silence while Martine thought about his reply. The rain was now falling softly and the thunder was gone. "I don't know what I think," Martine finally answered. You have...I have opened the door on a whole new panorama I never knew existed in me. Certainly it was never in my life before. I need to consider it carefully and not burn the bridge to the road going back. t.

"Then you are regretting what happened?" said Lance. "You didn't enjoy it the way I did?"

"Regret?" said Martine, questioningly. "Yes, I do regret it at this point, I think. As for enjoyment—as I have said to you so often in all the many times we've been together, Lance, we were not put in this world to surrender to the flesh."

"Geez, Martine, that's a lot of regret. It was a wild and wonderful male sexual encounter. Millions of men have them, enjoy the hell out of it and go about their lives. Even married men. It helps to let off a little steam."

"I can't do that," said Martine, shaking his head sadly. "Don't you see I can't be a priest of the church and break its laws, the eternal laws of God. I made a vow of chastity when I picked up the Cross of Jesus Christ to carry it and become his servant. And now...now I have broken that vow!"

"Oh, Martine, Martine. You're taking this too seriously. This has nothing to do with vows. It's just getting rid of tension. Other priests do this and think nothing of it. What do you bet?"

"Lance, I'm not other priests. I am Martine dePaul and my sole purpose in life has been to seek and work for a state of grace and while doing so serve both God and my fellow man. Just believe me when I tell you that the sins of the flesh offend and darken the soul. Anyway, I thought your weakness was women."

"Hey, don't get technical on me!" said Lance with a laugh. "Women are the greatest. I haven't seen one I couldn't bed. But sometimes when I've had a little to drink and I get real horny it can happen with a guy, especially if he's my buddy and I know he's feeling as affectionate as I am. Now, come on, Martine. I'm no faggot, if that's what you're thinking."

"Whatever the case, Lance, this cannot happen again," said Martine with finality.

"So, what are you going to do?" asked Lance, sliding down into the bed.

"I'm going to see that this never happens again. And this has nothing to do with you as a person. Physically, you are a picture of perfection. Just don't let that become your curse. My decision also does not mean I do not care. In fact, it dawned on me tonight that we have more than just a relationship, because I love you. With this realization, I am also aware that for the first time in my life I love someone physically."

"So where does that leave things?" asked Lance with a puzzled look.

"I haven't the foggiest," said Martine. "I guess it leaves me having to choose between love of the church or secular love, one or the other. It can't be both. Right now I choose to go to the bathroom."

"When you get back," yelled Lance, "I have an important question."

Knowing that it was closer to the six o'clock Mass than he cared to think, Martine took a quick shower. He returned with a towel tied around his waist. "Okay, what was the question, Lance?" he asked. There was no reply. Lance was sound asleep.

Martine said his evening prayers once again, uttering one of special contrition for a new sin he now felt weighing upon him. The prayer seemed lifeless, without spirit. He knew it went no further than the room. The prayer of the doomed and unforgiven sinner does not to Heaven rise. Wasn't there a line something like than in Hamlet, he thought.

Back in bed, Martine pulled the covers close against the slight chill and tried to think what he should do. The answers that came seemed to have no substance; and he could not clear from his thoughts some lines from Shelly that were still with him as he fell asleep:

"Life like a dome of many-colored glass
Stains the white radiance of Eternity."

Outside the rain had stopped and stars were visible between broken clouds racing over San Carlo.

I

The rain had left the world bright and pristine. Martine, on his way to celebrate Mass in San Luis Rey Church, noticed that even the village of San Carlo had the fresh appearance of yesterday rather than the aged face of its many centuries. He had left Lance still asleep. He wondered if there was any reason to talk further with him. The man, the boy, felt no remorse. His sunny nature seemed completely without guilt of any kind. This was truly the pagan view of the world and one's relationship to it, Martine concluded.

Even with the weight of the previous evening on his conscience, Martin felt a special sort of happiness this bright morning. It was reflected in the spring of his step, and in the way he looked forward to his duty in the church and the celebration of Mass. He had sensed real love for the first time and therein lay the struggle in which he now was trapped. If he was truly wed to the Holy Mother Church, was it possible to still hold in his heart the fleshly love of another human being? Already he knew the answer. But he still had to pursue it theologically, examine his true feelings minutely and perhaps seek the views of other people who knew and understood the church. One of those confidants was Father Fabian Chavez.

Why could he not deeply love someone platonically and this not conflict with his dedication to the church? He had once loved a girl in grammar school. That was platonic and did not result in lust or sin. Was the situation now not similar? he reasoned; yet, this was loving a man. In the Old Testament, David loved Jonathan and still loved God without reservation. Experiencing real love was like possessing everything of value in the world. But, suddenly Martine remembered the warning about gaining the whole world and losing one's own soul. Did he want to break his vow of poverty, also?

All these thoughts competed for his mind's attention, posing questions that must have answers if he was to be at peace with himself. But even if he had answers now, or found them in a lifetime, it still did not address the central issue in himself: how was he, a priest of the church—sworn to obey God and the church—capable of committing this particular offense? He would seek absolution from God. He would confess it to his father-confessor, Cipriano Montoya, the diocesan chancellor, who might demand his resignation as penance. Was he undergoing some moral decay that was weakening his defenses, making it possible, even desirable for him to play into the hands of lust? Would it happen again when he was off guard or did not have his defenses up?

No answers, not even shadowy ones, came to mind. Transcending this mental turmoil was the fleeting suspicion that this act might have welled up from his real and true nature.

Martine could see his mother, disappointed and suffering, willing to endure such a son simply because he was hers. With his father, it would be an entirely different matter. A son of this inclination would be a direct and personal affront to Edgar dePaul. He would have none of it. He would not have decadence and immorality in his presence; and there would be no stinting on expense or effort in sending such a son off to a clinic in a foreign land where the specialists, speaking in heavy accents, would be commissioned to cure him.

Martine could not allow himself to dwell further on the possibility that this single act came out of his true nature and had waited until this time in his life to make itself known. He was horrified by the prospect. He quickly opened one of the church's heavy wooden doors, touched the holy water and crossed himself. Here for the moment was refuge from the painful things that had reshaped his world in the last few hours. He moved toward the sacristy where Taegu was waiting with vestments.

Taegu was hesitant and jittery while helping Martine. Finally he mustered the courage to speak: "My mother came with me," he said. "She needs just a minute of your time before Mass, and we still have time, if it's okay?"

"Of course it is," said Martine. "Where is Lupe?"

Taegu opened the outside door to admit Guadalupe Quintana, a fat pleasant woman who allowed Martine to kiss her cheek.

"Lupe, how are you?" he asked. "I see you almost every day and always forget to tell you what a God-send Taegu is to the church. I don't know what I would do without him."

"Padre," said the dark smiling woman, "I thank you, but the reason I am here is that I have a message for you. The women of the village and some of the elders have asked me to tell you that you are the best priest we have had in a very long time. They hope you will stay many years because you have shown San Carlo that you are very...very...how do you say 'muy simp`atico'...nice to all of us and we like you."

Martine was visibly moved. "Thank you for coming to see me," he said. "Tell the village, as indeed I will, that I am most grateful and thankful for being allowed to serve you...all of you. Tell them I will always pray for the good of each of you and for San Carlo."

Lupe went into the church, leaving with Martine a basket of bread baked by the village women. He was saddened by this exhibit of acceptance and goodwill. He had now betrayed them as well as the church. They believed he was a servant of God, imbued with grace and goodness when in actuality he had committed a secret evil. His offense, as he characterized it in his mind, was haunting him. He imagined himself as a wolf in vestments pretending sanctity before sheep-like parishioners.

When Mass was over and he had shed his cassock and then sent Taegu home, Martine returned to the empty church and knelt before the altar where he repeated a psalm that always made him feel safe:

"Have mercy upon me, O God, according to thy loving kindness; according unto the multitude of thy tender mercies blot out my transgressions.

Wash me throughly from mine iniquity, and cleanse me from my sin.

For I acknowledge my transgressions; and my sin is ever before me.

Against thee, thee only, have I sinned, and done this evil in thy sight...."

That was just the point, he thought. His so-called offense was against God and the church, not against man, and this made it all the more terrible. He had harmed no other human being and therefore judgment and punishment would not come from mortals. If only it were that simple, he thought. To Martine it could be no worse than that.

Martine left the cool, dark interior and shielded his eyes against the morning sun, now well above the Sangre de Cristo Mountains. As he walked toward his studio he could see that the Jeep had disappeared.

Lance had left a note stuck to the refrigerator:

"Hey, Ole Buddy: Snap out of it. I had a great time. It was fantastic. You'll think better of it as the day goes by. By the way, I stole one of your beers. I'll call you. Lance."

Perhaps he would think better of it, but only in one way: when his very spirit felt that he had been absolved. He tried to think about preparing breakfast, but instead kept seeing Lance in his mind's eye, seeing him laughing and regretting nothing, full of youth and strength. He turned and looked out the window at the mountains beyond, whispering aloud to himself the words from an old Edith Piaff song: "Je ne regret rien."

Suddenly Martine was lonely. Oh, God, he said under his breath.

FIVE

San Carlo Pueblo, although close to Santa Fe, attracted very few tourists, even in a good season. Outside of the ancient church, there was little to draw visitors off the beaten path. San Carlo's handful of artisans, mostly pottery makers, had little choice but to join the other Indian merchants exhibiting under the portico of the sprawling Palace of the Governors facing Santa Fe's centuries-old plaza. Native craftsmen, sitting on blankets, had sold their jewelry, pottery and other offerings at this location time out of mind.

San Carlo pottery, fired to create a glossy, brick-red surface, was highly prized by collectors who usually paid top dollar. Martine was proud of the village potters and often gave them a ride to or from the plaza. As night gathered over the city, he now sat in his car waiting for three of them. The waiting did not bother him since the only thing on his agenda was a visit to Los Dos Tortugas where he was supposed to meet Lance in about an hour. Lance had called earlier from the ranch, and Martine was eager for young Cameron's company. It would be their first meeting since the stormy night, and Martine had come to some conclusions about what had happened and felt he could talk about it reasonably.

Life in the service of the church was not one of simplicity as he once imagined, because no matter how earnest his dedication, he had failed to keep his personal emotional shortcomings out of it. He looked toward the Palace for his villagers and briefly wished he could lead a life as uncomplicated as these people. But, then he remembered from his history that there was nothing very simple about them or their art or even this place where the artisans gathered.

Spain had spent more than two centuries in an effort to bring the native peoples under the rule of church and king. The massive Palace of the Governors was built as part of the subjugation effort. The royal governor, Pedro de Peralta, had ordered its construction in 1610 as the principal administrative office of Spanish Government in Nueva Viscaya's new capital, La Villa Real de la Santa Fe de San Francisco. The first Spanish capital, at nearby San Gabriel for most of a century, had been too difficult to defend against the hostile native warriors. Construction on the new capital took place at a time when wilderness ruled most of the American continent except for the tiny British enclave of Jamestown, Virginia, where Europeans were barely holding on by their fingernails.

Time had trodden heavily here, Martine thought. This building had seen rebellions, conspiracies leading to revolt, reconquest, war and civil war; and across the street in the plaza it had seen the horrors of man's cruelty: executions by beheading and garroting of men who opposed the government, and the use of whipping and the stocks for natives who did not follow the rules. Suddenly, his train of thought was broken by the arrival of his passengers, three San Carlo women.

■

Lance held up two fingers to a waiter in the distance as Martine sat down in their usual booth. "Bring two beers," he called out above the din of the early evening crowd. "I'm glad you came," he said turning to Martine.

"And, I'm even happier you called," replied Martine. "I was beginning to wonder if you'd had second thoughts about our relationship, about what happened."

"Second thoughts, Old Buddy? Me?" Lance smiled broadly. "I only have first thoughts and I act on them, and I'm generally right that first time. No, in fact we've been doing a lot of fencing on the north range, and it's kept me tied down for nearly a week. What about yourself? Has your outlook on things changed? I know Mom and Sis have seen you at Mass and Mom said you looked good?

"Looked good?" said Martine with a start. "You asked your mother how I looked? You want to raise doubts with your family?"

"No, nothing like that. Mom just volunteered the report in an off-handed way. Nothing was meant by it. Quit being so jittery. What I do, what we do, is no one's business but ours. Why would anyone care unless they had a sick mind?"

"Perhaps I am too sensitive; but you've got to realize my life has taken a turn and I'm still adjusting to it, sorting things out. You, on the other hand, seem to see nothing unusual about what happened. Give me some slack, as they say, Lance. You know I can't be nonchalant about this."

"Now, Martine," said Lance with a wide smile, "whenever was making love to someone cause for alarm, unless it was rape or something, or prostitution? I thought that loving was one of the things we were supposed to do in this crazy world of ours."

The drink made Martine feel better, but he was disappointed that the conversation seemed to be going wrong, following the same old pattern: he the moralist and Lance the pagan. He wanted to deal with truths, not positions on morality.

"Look, Lance," he said, drawing himself up against the table, "I will give you the truth only as I know it. You could expect nothing less of me as your parish priest and as a friend. The other night—afterward—you asked me what I thought and I couldn't tell you. I was shocked at myself—not you, so much—but at myself for what I had allowed to happen because it felt good; and I was shocked that I had broken faith with God and with the church, because I have sworn a vow of chastity; and I also was shocked to discover that I had in me the propensity, the tendency, to do what I did. I never knew before that it was there—not in my wildest imagination.

"So, Lance, this much I know as fact because I now have a clear picture. I have committed a grave offense for which I am doing contrition and which I must confess to my father-confessor. I cannot begin to guess what will be my punishment. On the other hand, you, Lance, have broken no vow, but you have broken the laws of God and of the church, and I would hope you would renounce all such acts and seek to atone for your sins."

"Holy hell, Padre," sputtered Lance with an affronted look, "You're actually going to sit down and tell someone in a collar what we did? You're going to tell him something that is private between us."

"Whoa, whoa, Lance. I didn't say I was going to use your name. That's not in the nature of the confession; but I am bound by my office and by reason of being a Catholic to confess all my sins, this one in particular. That doesn't mean I relate all the details."

"God! I would hope not," gasped Lance with a sigh of relief. "Look," he said, lighting two cigarettes at the same time and handing one to Martine. "Let me offer something." His smile was returning now. "I, too, will deal in facts. You are older, have your education and hold a responsible place in the world, but that doesn't mean that your interpretation of everything is always the unshakable truth. I think your position on what amounted to nothing more than having a little male fun is totally out of the ball park. You're reading too much into it. We had fun. We didn't harm anyone and that's that. Where's the sin and the guilt and all that punishment stuff? Who, besides you, says so?"

"Holy Mother Church says so."

"But, Buddy, these are old men just making up rules for someone else to follow. I know a little bit about what some of the popes used to do, what some of the priests still do and what people like Lot and David did. Hey, man, I have never done anything like that, nor have you. Most of these rules are made up by someone else who has already done all this stuff and now they don't want anyone else to have any fun. I haven't killed anyone, beat anyone up or hurt anyone and I don't see where I have anything to regret."

There was that word regret again, thought Martine as he said, "Lance, I understand clearly the point you are trying to make. In many ways you are a fine human being, a beautiful person, and there's great potential in that magnificent temple of yours. But...."

"Ah, here's the 'but'," interrupted Lance.

"But, all those good qualities don't make a human being that is totally acceptable to God. Leading a life of sexual promiscuity is a grievous error that can lose you the Kingdom of Heaven."

"But you don't know about love, Martine. You told me so. You have never made love to a woman. So how can you comprehend what's involved here?"

"There's intuitive understanding based on certain facts we have learned, Lance. For example, without ever having fallen from a cliff, you know the result if you should have such a fall: you'll be either killed or badly maimed, depending on how far you fall and on what type of material you may land. You're right, I have never made love to a woman, but I also know that the physical act is not love, but lust and a thing of the flesh. To be in love in the true sense, there must be a number of other factors including commitment, sharing and the keeping of obligations."

"So, then," asked Lance earnestly, "what are you going to do? What do you think our relationship is?"

"No matter what you may think, Lance, what we did was wrong, very wrong. At least for me it was. I want this aspect of our future to be very clear to both of us. As for how I feel about you, there is little doubt in my mind that it can be anything other than love.

"This is not something I willed to happen. It just happened. How did Emily Dickinson put it: 'The soul selects her own society.' How odd it is that we seem to have so little control over who we ultimately love." He could see that Lance appeared uncomfortable, but he continued. "There is one last thing you must know. I am not certain that a priest of the church can serve two masters: one, love of and obedience to the church and love—even platonically—of another human being, especially one of the same sex.

"That's just the way it is, Lance, and it's not necessarily of my choosing." Martine gave a small laugh, but Lance did not seem amused as he continued talking. "If the verdict goes against my emotional equation, then I have a last and final decision to make. I must choose between what I feel for you and what I feel for the church. Lance, it shatters me to say that should this happen, there is only one path I can choose, and you know what it is—the church."

Their conversation was interrupted by the waiter who brought two more beers. Martine had been matching Lance's pace, and he was feeling the resulting warm glow.

Suddenly, out of the shadows came a wizened old woman with a toothless smile who pushed in beside Lance and sat down. She had straight, stringy hair that fell from under a man's dark battered hat. Her jeans and denium jacket were faded, and her wrinkled, brown fingers held a twisted pinch of cigarette that gave off an acrid smoke. Martine could see she was quite drunk.

"This is Bonnie," said Lance. "Meet Martine."

"That's Bonnie Peña to you, young priest," she said. "My friends call me Old Bonnie, but you ain't my friends."

Martine was startled that the old woman knew him. "How do you know what I do?"

"Bonnie knows everybody," Lance said. "She's a member of our art colony here."

"I've been here on this desert longer than any of 'em," she said, "even before your pa was born, Mr. Big Rancher Cameron. Why don't you buy Old Bonnie a beer? You buy for everybody else."

Lance held three fingers up toward the bar.

Martine thought the woman looked like one of the avenging furies of mythology. Wrinkles radiated around her lips like cracks in the bark of an aged tree.

She looked at Lance through glassy eyes and said, "So you got one of your boyfriends with you, eh?"

"Now Bonnie," Lance said in exasperation, "you know better than that. Martine is a priest, the priest of San Luis Rey Church."

But Bonnie's voice took on an insidious tone, Martine thought. "Now, fellas, you don't fool old Bonnie," she cackled. "I seen you two in here before and I could tell by the way he looked at you, Mr. Rancher, that you two were making the 'beast with two backs' as old Shakespeare put it.

Lance was now irritated. "Now, Bonnie, I want you to knock off the bull shit. That's just about enough. I think you'd do well to start minding your own business.

"Well, you don't need to get huffy with Old Bonnie," she said. "Why should I care if you're doing it. I used to have girlfriends and boyfriends, too. They all thought I was something in those days." Her cackle grew louder and she added, "Yeah, you don't fool Old Bonnie."

Martine could feel the warmth of humiliation on his face. This woman, drunken and perhaps demented, he thought, was closer to the truth than she perhaps realized. He wondered if it was that obvious and glanced quickly up and around the lounge to see if anyone was watching. The woman's scratchy voice and broken laughter were growing louder. "Yes, sir, you can't fool Old Bonnie. I know boyfriends when I sees 'um."

A sharp crack split the air as Lance snapped his fingers, drawing Poncho's attention at the bar. The bartender glanced only once in Lance's direction and came immediately. "Okay, Bonnie," he said firmly. "Let's move it. One more word and you're out of here. You know better than bother the guests." Poncho's strong hand reached for the old woman, but she shrugged it off and shuffled away.

"I'm sorry, Padre," Poncho apologized. "She gets like that when she's been drinking all day. I hope you won't hold that against us," he said before turning away.

"What in the world was that all about?" asked a visibly shaken Martine. "She was completely out of it."

"Old Bonnie's like that," said a solemn Lance. "She's always been a little wacko. We used to run from her when we were kids because all the Hispanic folks called her La Bruja...that's Spanish for The Witch. She was a painter, still is. She lives up in the hills near here."

"But what she said...does she claim to be a seer, you know, clairvoyant? Those shots weren't wild, they were near-misses. Too close for comfort."

"Hey, forget it, hear?" said Lance, trying to dismiss the incident. "Go to some of the galleries over on Canyon Road sometime and see a few of her paintings. She sells them."

"What are they like?" asked Martine.

"Oh, I don't know. They're dark things—paintings of the underworld in mythology, portraits of Lucifer and the devil doing various things. I think I remember one because it was a real horror painting. You know, the devil devouring people, or something like that."

Martine shivered. "It sounds like the very thing for the living room," he laughed. Lance seemed morose and gloomy. "Look," Martine continued, "I'm the only one who seems to have a problem, or at least I reflect on it as such. It's not something you can do anything about. As they say in the vernacular, I will have to find my own salvation.

"If I can give you nothing else, Lance, I can offer moral support and the spiritual guidance I have been trained to give all people. And if it is any help, comfort to you, we will always have our friendship. I mean sincere and lasting friendship. It lasts a lifetime, forever, and it means that if one is a friend they will come to the aid of their friend in need by traveling whatever miles, by enduring whatever hardships and by giving whatever support is needed—no matter how much."

"That's quite a commitment," said Lance ordering another beer. "You know, we're about to get smashed. But it helps me to find the words to tell you how I really feel. Let me ramble on and get it off my chest. You have given me more than I have given you. I feel I have nothing to give. I haven't been to a big name school and I'm not sophisticated like you are. Your interests run in different directions from mine, so sometimes I feel that you have just tagged along, kinda, just to humor me. Maybe you even hoped to change me in some way, although I feel no need of being changed.

"Well, that's not the point I'm trying to make. I owe it to you to be candid, truthful even if it hurts, and I don't want you to get me wrong. I don't love other people in the way you do, so I can't return what you are offering—the way you feel about me. I'm sorry, I don't love anyone. So, I guess when all is said and done, I'm guilty of using you for my own benefit. That's my fault. I didn't intend for it to turn out this way."

Martine was stunned by this revelation. It brought to mind the words of someone whose name he could not remember: "A life of pleasure kills all capacity for love." Perhaps that was Lance's undoing, his fatal flaw. "Lance," he said sadly, "that's all right. People only give what they are capable of giving."

"I've got a lot still to think about," said Lance, apparently intending to end the conversation, "and I've a lot of work to do tomorrow. The summer is going fast." He rose and extended his hand to Martine, and there seemed to be an air of finality about his departure. "Hey, if I've hurt you, I'll make it up to you. I need to think." And he was gone.

Martine suddenly felt very alone, a sensation seldom present in his emotions. Something in him wanted to call out, "Lance, don't go. Come back and be with me." This was absurd, he told himself. He leaned his head back against the booth and tossed down the rest of his beer. I will not be ruled by emotions, he told himself decisively. Yet, the longing was there. His terrible desire was awake and moving, pacing back and forth in its cage.

Martine went straight home instead of to the old church to say his nightly offices. Why did it not bother him that he failed to do this? He was almost afraid to search out and identify an answer, but the answer was pushing its attentions on him, and he did not like its message. His spiritual core, always so firm and unwavering to all outward evils was disintegrating from within. He visualized a wooden pillar, its outward appearance undisturbed and solid, while internally voracious termites tunneled throughout the structure.

The mystery and magnificence of the Mass now moved him less. The once poignant sorrow he felt for the world's cruelty to the crucified Christ was diminished. He felt a lagging confidence in himself as a servant of the church and God. He reasoned that if he had done something so completely sinful and unworthy then by what right was he still worthy to celebrate the Mass, utter the prayer of consecration, touch the blessed Body and Blood of Christ Himself. He had to see Father Montoya.

Looking in his mirror and feeling the effects of the alcohol, he tried to see if his features were changing. He imagined it could be like the story of Dorian Gray in reverse—that instead of a painted portrait somewhere changing to reflect his sins, it was his own face that was engraved with evil. Down deep he knew that this was not true. He could see that his was still the unblemished face it always was. Tomorrow he would call Monsignor Montoya's office for an appointment. Meantime, he would beseech God to stay the evil that was gaining on him and to reignite the old spiritual flame that had burned so brightly for most of his youth.

But Martine did not call Monsignor Montoya. It was not that he had reservations about making his confession. That was an obligation, stated and agreed to when he first arrived in Santa Fe and was given the diocesan briefing. The man was too haughty, arrogant and overbearing for the office he held, tending to treat those beneath his rank with ill-disguised contempt.

On their first meeting, the diocesan chancellor had been rudely forward, telling the young priest, "We have heard quite a lot about you, father. It appears that you have greatly impressed his Eminence, Cardinal Monahan, with your piety and devotion. We want it understood that in this archdiocese all members of the priesthood are regarded equally, and no one is accorded any special recognition because he exercises either real or pretended adoration for things of the church, or practices special reverence in his personal conduct. These attributes are expected of all priests and they elicit no special consideration or favors from this office or that of the most reverend archbishop. This office affords no one any special preference."

"Monsignor, I would expect to be treated the same as all other members of this sacred fraternity," Martine had replied.

Ignoring his response, Montoya had continued: "And there is one thing further. We are aware of the special, shall we say rapport, that exists between his eminence and yourself. We would caution you that your status as a protege of the cardinal should not encourage you to seek advantage from that status, or to communicate to his eminence any report of matters that pertain to the governance of this archdiocese. We would take an exceedingly dim view of any such activity, and it would not escape our attention."

Martine had told himself that Monsignor Montoya was the type of church official that must have been chosen as grand inquisitor during the Spanish church's inquisition against heresy.

This assessment caused Martine to delay what he feared would be an unpleasant encounter, and he could not begin to imagine the monsignor's reaction to his inevitable confession. Even though the confessional was inviolate, shielded from all but the priest's ears, he could not picture relating an offense such as his to a confessor with Montoya's towering hauteur.

Meanwhile he had decided that as a preliminary to facing Montoya, he would confide in two people he could count on as being sympathetic, no matter how grave, no matter how devastating: Dalrymple, a known member of the gay community, and Father Fabian who always had words of comfort for all people regardless of the severity of their transgressions.

First, however, he felt compelled for reasons not clear in his thinking to contact Lance one more time. He telephoned Cameron Ranch several times, but each time Amanda had told him her son was out on horseback at some remote spot on the big spread. She had taken messages, but they were not returned; and once on the weekend, Martine had gone to Los Dos Tortugas searching without success. It was clear that he was being avoided. Toward the end of the second week, Martine drove to the familiar tavern once again and this time the Jeep with the Three-J trademark was there.

Lance and Cindi sat in the usual booth. It was apparent from Lance's flushed face that he had already downed a number of rounds.

"Hey, Old Buddy!" Lance called as he motioned Martine to the seat facing the couple, "It's time you got here. I just called your number and there was no answer."

"He did do that, you gorgeous married man," added Cindi with a tilt of her head.

"Lance, I've called you at the ranch several times and left my number with your mother. You don't return your calls."

"Come on, man, you know what Amanda is like. She likely wrote your number down some place in her notebook and then forgot about it by the time I got home. She's always on the run and wouldn't remember that I was supposed to return calls." Turning to Cindi with a laugh, he asked "How's that for a complicated explanation?"

"That's the best I've heard, Hon," she replied; "But as I said awhile ago, I've got to go over to my sister's. She'll be wondering what happened to me because I promised her I would come over tonight." Getting up she added, "Now you guys can do whatever it is that guys do." She tapped Lance on the mouth and turned briskly away.

"So, why were you calling me? asked Lance.

"I wanted us to meet and talk, and, I guess, just sort of be together," said Martine hesitantly, as he took a long drink from the beer Lance had ordered. "Isn't that the normal thing friends do?" He was having a hard time giving the right start to the conversation and the distant look on Lance's face wasn't helping to build his courage.

"I've been out on the far range for nearly two weeks, now," Lance said. "That's upland country, in the mountains. At that altitude the growth is something like New England's. Lots of hardwoods, pines, grass and in wet weather there are little streams everywhere. You can get off your horse and just sit there and think—sometimes it feels like something a fellow could do all day and not move or get hungry or anything. And it gets more beautiful in September when the aspens begin turning. You'll have to go out then and get my dad to take you up there. I'll be back in the university by then. Oh, Martine, it's so quiet up there—you can't hear one sound of civilization. It must be like most of the country was before men came to screw everything up.

"I suppose this is a long way of getting around to saying that I had an opportunity to do that thinking I promised you. Up there in that country, it's just you and your mind, your other self and you can think so clearly and see things so clearly. It's like having another person, a quiet person, to bounce things off. Maybe when you're up there like that and can see so far, your mind clears. I don't know. Does that make any sense?"

"So, what did you think about?" asked Martine.

"I thought about us and all the things that have happened to us during this long summer; how we met as strangers and got to know one another and shared all the ideas we both had; and how we finally shared ourselves. I thought of how it was great for me but caused you nothing but anguish. I'm in agreement with you—I don't want it to happen again for your sake, your well being."

"It won't," said Martine assertively.

But Martine was shaken by Lance's quick reply. "It could," he said. "I would go right now with a little prompting because I don't place any kind of moral value on that kind of fooling around. But you, on the other hand, might not have the will power to resist...you know drinking and everything. Then you'd be twice as miserable. You'd have to go through all that self-examination again. What do you call it—recriminations. Hey, that only makes you miserable afterward. Neither of us can guarantee it wouldn't happen again." After a pause, he smiled and said, "You see, I can tell you what I really think."

Martine admitted to himself that although he had said never again, he hadn't really come to grips with the question of his will power. He had failed before. Could he trust himself? It remained a question.

"So, Lance, you seem to have reached some decision, some conclusion?"

"It's obvious to both of us," Lance said unsmiling. "Our relationship can lead nowhere except into hurt for you. You have an emotional attachment for me—something that I cannot return. I have a tremendous sexual appetite that isn't too choosy when it comes to having fun, and you want no part of that. Where does that leave us? Polls apart, that's where.

"You're a nice guy, Martine; and if anyone is really into the church thing you seem to be the perfect person—ideal. God only knows, I don't want to hurt you any further. So, then, it's not my decision but the only thing that makes sense. It all comes down to the fact that after we take stock of ourselves and each other, we have nothing in common. By not spending time together, we will run no further risks."

Lance's words cut a large hole that Martine felt suddenly gaping in the pit of his stomach. The hurt caused him to gasp. "You're not intentionally hurting me. It's a situation that developed because I couldn't firmly, adamantly resist temptation. I think I have known all along that I had to decide between the world of the flesh and that of the spirit. I have simply procrastinated. We never want to give up the person we love most.

"Because we are friends, Lance, I will confide in you my most troubling secret. I don't understand my emotional attachment for you. How can one man love another—physically that is. I am appalled to find this thing in myself. If I let it go, gave it rein, it could become an obsession; and as far as I can determine, it could push everything else out of life. Do you know what I'm saying?"

"The shadow that had lain over Lance's face lifted. "I know, but I don't understand it either," he said in a tone of bafflement. "I know that there are men, and women too, who love people of the same sex. It happens among gay people, and these guys have the same commitment as heterosexual people have. Some even get married."

"Do you think I am gay, and have never confronted it before?" asked Martine sadly.

"Have you ever felt this way before about another man?"

"No! Not ever. That's why this comes as such a shock."

"Well, of course, that doesn't tell either one of us anything. You can't ask me. You need to talk to an expert. Maybe it happens now and then that perfectly normal people, just once in their lives, can fall in love with someone of the same sex. I don't have a scientific answer, not a clue. I don't know if there is one.

"If I am truthful with myself, I guess I have been pretty selfish with you, Martine. I've known how you felt about me for some time, now, and it flattered me. I guess I played to it, knowing all along that I didn't feel the same way. Up there on the high range it came to me as plain as day that this situation is hurting you and your work. I really do have something of a conscience, believe it or not. I wouldn't want to think that I was responsible for another person giving up or losing heart for their career, even if it is for the church on which I'm not awfully sold."

Lance paused and looked at his watch. "It's that time," he said. "Walk me out."

They paused at the Jeep and Lance turned to Martine. "Don't ask," he said, "I can drive. My mind seems to have cleared."

He moved closer to Martine. "Take my hand. We'll always be friends, Martine. I can't guarantee you how good my end of it will be. I know my interest-span isn't long and I don't sustain affection very well. My track record isn't good, but...friends?"

In a weak voice Martine answered, "Friends." He stood in the Jeep's headlights and watched Lance drive away.

SIX

Santa Fe is a city of churches and their variety and uniqueness were a thing of wonder for Martine, especially San Miguel Mission, America's oldest church, built by Franciscans in the first decade of the seventeenth century. Standing to the side of the Old Santa Fe Trail, it was a structure he could not avoid passing each time he visited Dalrymple on Canyon Road.

The smell of tempera paints filled the studio as the painter handed Martine a beer, lit a cigarette and continued working on a large canvas, still holding his part of the conversation. "From the look on your face I'd say you want to discuss something other than music for the Sunday Mass," said Dalrymple. "Where's your sidekick, Lance?"

"I don't know," said Martine. "At the ranch, I suppose. I haven't seen him in several days. Why do you ask?"

"Well, I haven't seen him at Mass with his mother in some time and people have seen the two of you round about in Santa Fe. Have you finished making a true believer out of that young renegade, and now it's time to rest and recuperate? I'd think anyone who tackled that task would need a rest. But then conversion is a specialty with you Franciscan brothers, isn't it?"

"Converting the heathen is only a tiny part of our work," Martine said with a smile of irony. "That aside, Dal, I need to talk, confide in you. You know those of us wearing the collar are always listening, but then there comes a time when we need to have someone listen to us, but I don't want to impose on you."

"God, is it that bad?" asked Dalrymple, putting aside his brush, coated with globs of yellow and brown. "You know you can talk to me about anything. I am like your other self."

"I don't know where to start...my life has become so complicated."

"Start at the beginning."

"Maybe I should say first," muttered Martine, clearing his throat uncomfortably, that I felt you would know where I'm coming from since you have tried to lighten your burden by telling me something about your own problems.

"Dal, I've discovered something about myself that has shattered me. It has left my soul in torment. It is destroying me and my work, bit by bit; and I have no peace of mind. I think...I believe...there are some things that point to my being gay!"

"You're what?" said his friend with an exploding laugh. You're gay, you think you're gay? So what? It's a way of life. I've been there these forty odd years as have millions of other people?"

"Come on! I'm dead serious, and it's nothing to laugh about."

"Martine, I'm not laughing about that. You should see your face. I thought you had cancer or even worse—only weeks to live. It was a laugh of relief, if anything."

"Dal, you know enough about the church to grasp why I'm hurting. No offense to you, but let me put it the way I see my situation. Here I am, a priest of the Holy Catholic Church, sworn to uphold its teachings and sworn to practice them in my private life, to pursue purity, decency, and chastity; and by example help others walk in that direction. Now, what kind of example can be set by a priest who is gay? By his very nature he is a rebuke to the teachings of the church...."

"Wait, hold it a minute," Dalrymple interrupted with a wave of his hand. "Let's go one step at a time. How do you suddenly know you're gay? Did this revelation come in a dream, a bolt of lightning, what?"

Martine, always comfortable in his conversations with Dalrymple, had thought this disclosure would be simple, but now he felt mortified. "I find without knowing why that I am physically attracted to someone of my own sex," he said awkwardly. "If the emotion isn't carnal love, then it's an awfully good imitation. Dal, I have studied psychology and taken courses in all kinds of related fields, but I honestly did not know that such a thing—such an emotion for one's own sex—was possible."

"It's not an imitation," said Dalrymple with a knowing smile. "It's the genuine article. It's love when you feel it, when you want to be with that person, when you want to imitate what they do, when you want to touch them, have them close to you. Although, with young men or young women, at some point in their lives, there can be an infatuation for someone of their own sex and it may never happen again and may not be a manifestation of a permanent homosexual orientation. Did you act on this urge in any way?"

Martine felt a warm flush going over him, as if naked before the world. He searched for words. "How can I tell you this—portray it so you will understand it exactly. I do not want to color the incident so it might be misleading."

Again Dalrymple broke in. "Let me help you. Did you make the first advance?"

"No, it came unexpectedly, almost by accident from the other person. To begin with I had had too much to drink, and when this person was having chills from getting soaked in the rain storm, he persuaded me that body heat would help him recover. Dal, I can't believe I was so naive? He relieved himself by massaging his body against mine and I acquiesced."

"He was the aggressor, then?" said Dalrymple, his knowing smile more pronounced.

"Yes, but I am equally guilty. I gave in to it. I will make no excuses. I was a party to wickedness and through this lust—this mortal sin—committed yet another sin. I broke my vow of chastity. So, there it is. You can see what's eating on me."

"Afterward, what did this other person say?" asked Dalrymple. "Did he offer an explanation?"

"He later said it was just fooling around, that he had gotten horny, I think he said, and that it was just a male sex thing that millions of people do."

Dalrymple slapped his knee with one hand and tossed his head to the side as he shouted, "That damn Lance! That SOB!"

"I didn't say who it was," protested Martine, his face frozen in surprise.

"You didn't have to. That's his M.O. Half the county knows about him. He's been seducing both boys and girls since he was sixteen and the hell of it is that he's so damned handsome that they let him— sometimes even ask for it. I should have warned you about him. He saw you—a vulnerable young priest—coming. He took advantage of you and to him it was just another conquest. That young fellow has the moral restraint of an alley cat. All along he was charming and leading you on, making you believe he was fertile ground in which you could plant the seed of a future dedicated Catholic. Oh, Martine, Martine. I'm sorry this happened to you, of all people."

"Please, Dal," Martine implored, "forget Lance's name in connection with this. You can see that if Amanda Cameron heard such a thing about her son she would be desolate. What I'm telling you has to be about me and me alone."

"Okay, Martine," said Dalrymple with resignation, "but I can assure you that Amanda Cameron cannot be unaware of the wide path her son has cut as he sowed his wild oats. Like many protective mothers she might deny the truth to outsiders, even to herself, but she knows. Down deep she knows."

"Anyway, Dal, I have pretty much drawn you the picture. I'm not being melodramatic when I tell you that these two things—discovery of myself and breaking my vow—have shattered me. Of course I must confess these things to the church, but that doesn't do much for my conscience right now. Even after I do penance and I am absolved of these transgressions, breaking my vow will still haunt me. Knowing what my true nature is also will haunt me. How can I serve as a virtuous example? That's dishonest, totally dishonest. I'm sure you didn't expect such a disclosure from your parish priest."

"Martine, you're going too fast for me to keep up with the points you are making," said Dalrymple. "As I said before, let's address them one at a time. First, let's take your discovery of what you think is your sexual orientation. If you really are gay, how can you place a guilt label on that? You're not guilty of anything."

"It's an unnatural affection," said Martine. "Besides, it's a complication I don't need in my life. You, of all people, know the wall of contempt and prejudice that gay people must face in our world."

"Martine, calm down," soothed Dalrymple. "I know this incident comes as a shock, but, Padre, Padre, Padre, one such incident is in no way a standard by which we can judge someone as homosexual or that they are destined to that orientation. But for argument's sake, let's say you were gay and in the priesthood. What of it? You would still be subject to the vow of chastity—no sexual encounter of any sort with anyone, no matter if they were women or men. So, how does it make a difference? It seems to me there's no issue here.

Further, who's to know about this? Are you planning to make an announcement from the pulpit, put up posters, what?"

"Think about it, Dal. My superiors are going to know as soon as I make my confession to my father-confessor."

"Then don't confess it. By whose rule is it a sin in the first place?"

"You suggest that I knowingly practice deceit? Dal, you know better! As a man thinketh in his heart, so is he."

"Where's the deceit?" Dal sputtered. "Do people go in and say, 'Father, forgive me for I have sinned. I'm a heterosexual?' Of course they don't. So why should you be confessing a different orientation? Huh? Tell me?"

"It's a question of integrity, Dal."

"Look, Martine! I'm not a theologian, but I just don't see this purple transgression you are nailing yourself to a cross for. Not only are some priests gay, they even practice being gay and apparently think nothing about it."

"That's just it, Dal," said Martine with furrowed brow. "They don't think about it. They have no conscience. I could not live like that. It would be like wearing the uniform of your country but working all the while for the country's enemies. No, no, never."

"Maybe you are one of those rare people who came into the world in a state of grace and only viewed the face of sin. As a result you are torturing yourself needlessly. I happen to think you are a good person. But, then, I can't give you 'church' answers. Many of those answers I can't agree with because they don't make any sense.

"If it'll be of any help to you, I'll tell you about my own self discovery when I was about fourteen or fifteen years old. I was in high school and I had class with a well dressed young fellow who had blond hair and blue eyes. To my way of thinking, he was worldly, knew his way around in all kinds of situations and pretty soon I found myself admiring everything about him. Then one day—it was toward the end of the school year—I was in the hallway and I saw him coming down the stairs from the second floor. And right then and there it struck me like a thunderbolt: what I was feeling for him was 'Love' with the capital 'L.'

"I couldn't believe it. I had never heard of such a thing. And, of course, I dared not tell this young man, this boy, what I was feeling. Oh, it was a powerful feeling. I tried to dress like him, I wanted to work at the same type of job that he held and for a while even tried to train my hair style like his. I mean I was completely envious of everything about him.

"Well, he kind of tolerated me. I think I inveigled him once into going with me to a movie that had Donald O'Connor in it. We never had a date or anything like that. The truth is, I had never heard of such an arrangement between guys. I tried to communicate how much I admired him and all that sort of thing; and one day when I was chattering on in this manner, he looked at me and said with a rebuff I'll never forget, 'What the heck do you want me to do, put my arms around you?' Of course I was embarrassed and didn't have any answer.

"I had a bad time of it when he finally joined the Navy. He once sent me a postcard from the Great Lakes Naval Training Station. The feeling gradually faded. Years later I ran into him again and we had a couple of beers. I was flabbergasted at what a bum he was. I thought once or twice of telling him how I had felt about him when I was a teenager, just to see his reaction; but then I thought better of it. He wouldn't have understood, being the redneck that he really was."

"So that's how you found out?" asked Martine.

"That's about it," said Dalrymple. "And it's one of the loneliest feelings in the world when you're a kid. You feel all alone in a strangeness that you don't dare reveal to anyone, especially that best friend you have the crush on. That would put him out of your life forever, and after he told everyone in the community you would be the town freak. That's the price a kid often has to pay for loving someone. It's one of the incredible quirks of our society that sometimes the teenager fares better if he beats another guy up. Then he might be considered a hero. Why is society like that? I don't know. Maybe if I had a lifetime to spend on research I could come up with some answers."

"Why have I just now found out what you learned at fourteen?" puzzled Martine?

"I don't know that you have," said Dalrymple. "The fact that this comes along when you are nearly twice the age I was is a good indication that it's one of those odd twists of your human nature, a passing thing that might never happen to you again.

"It continued to happen to me after that first time. And, indeed, you do ask at some point, 'why me?' The hell of it is, though, that after I experienced that first crush, even after several of them, I didn't know enough to put my finger on it, identify what was happening to me. I just kept quiet and figured it was my lot in life. Then when I was about seventeen or eighteen, I met an older guy who had been to college and out in the world and somehow he got on the subject of ancient Sparta and how love was practiced between that country's warriors.

"Well, that was my opportunity to ply him with questions and he assured me to my amazement that this had been happening since time began. He went on to explain that it often involved sexual relations and the whole nine yards just as in relationships between men and women. He assured me it was not an unusual custom. Yes, he had an ulterior motive. He later tried without much success to demonstrate his lecture. I just wasn't ready for the sex business, although by then I had had a crush on at least half a dozen good-looking young friends."

"It's a cruel discovery for a person of any age," Martine said glumly. "The pity is, that there is so little information available for young people. There's virtually nowhere they can turn to get advice and comfort."

"That's partly because of churchmen like yourself," laughed Dalrymple. "No offense intended, but they, along with much of the leadership in most societies, have made the whole topic taboo. It's like the subject of sex itself. It has had virtually no serious scientific study. Wouldn't you think that since mankind perpetuates itself through sex that it would be a separate field of inquiry in medicine and psychology like, say, blood, anatomy, diseases and the like? No way. Slap a thin coating of 'sin' on it and the topic of sex almost becomes invisible.

"The experts who count noses believe that ten percent of any given population has this orientation. Down through the centuries the gay population has numbered in its ranks kings and generals, great writers and painters, scientists and farmers and, yes, even a president of the United States."

"I agree with much of your reasoning," said Martine, "but I live and minister in that portion of the society that finds the gay orientation unaccepable. It is, in fact, unacceptable to me, personally. If it should turn out that this is my nature, then I shall have to find a way of living with it. Dal, I can never, never accept it because the church's teaching does not condone it as a way of life. As a priest, I have no prejudice toward it and will follow the church's teaching in regard to the gay lifestyle; and you already know, Dal, the church views the practice as a mortal sin. Therefore that is also what I believe."

"Well, Padre, that's why we gay people so often have to develop theology to meet our own needs," said Dalrymple with a smile, "else how could we survive in a hostile environment?"

He picked up a heavy white cloth and went to the painting and carefully draped it over the easel and unfinished canvass. He continued talking as he opened a small refrigerator and took out two beers. "Martine, I guess about the only way I can sum up any kind of answer to your discovery is to say that for millions of people who come into this world with that orientation, it's the only life they have and they would be hard put to regard themselves as sinful because of it. You, on the other hand, are involved in a morality struggle with your nature, if indeed that is your nature. I can only suggest that you might find some kind of answer by talking with a Catholic theologian, and as you know Father Fabian is still one of the best."

"I had definitely planned to see him after talking with you," Martine said quietly.

"Whatever you do, Martine," urged Dalrymple, "don't even think of a thing like leaving the church, the priesthood. I think you were born for it and your influence on people is fantastic from everything I can see. I can see the change you have brought about at San Luis Rey. More and more people are coming back just because of you and the new spirit you have generated among all of us. As for this broken vow thing, certainly I would think it can be repaired through contrition. Listen to me. I sound like a father-advisor."

"I'm tired," said Martine getting up from his chair. "So much thinking makes one tired. I'm going home and sleep on it. After I talk with Father Fabian maybe I'll have a better idea. I'll certainly need one when I see the chancellor. Montoya is strictly a no-nonsense cleric."

Dalrymple extended his hand and said, "Good luck."

Back in his studio Martine found himself far from sleep. He remembered that he had failed to visit the old church for his final prayers. Instead he opened his personal missal and knelt at a portable altar in his studio. He ended his devotional with his own prayer, composed of words that grew out of the pain and turmoil inside him:

"Oh, God, I do not ask much and want very little. I ask only that a true and contrite spirit be renewed in me and that it will serve to overcome the alien nature that has stirred in my heart. Cover me with Thy hand and shield me from all evil. Protect me from this thing that is not of my devising and lead me that I may serve and do Thy will. This I ask in the name of Jesus Christ, Thy Son, who came into the world to save sinners."

He then placed a Mozart trio in his tape player, sat down and thought about his visit and discussion with Dalrymple. Dal's views did nothing to put his dilemma in perspective or produce any kind of answer that was reassuring. If anything, his story about his own evolving youth was rather like taking a penciled outline and painting in a full, clear portrait of the self Martine saw in his own mind and detested.

Martine got up, opened a beer and took down several books, including a poetry collection. He was restless, the evening incomplete. Then the realization struck him: he was what was incomplete. He felt the need to be with and in the company of the person he loved. What a damnable, ludicrous desire, he told himself. He leafed through a collection of poems. He remembered the poem, 'Wild Plum' by Orrick Johns, a forgotten American poet, long dead. It was about people who are doomed to love the exotic, little known beauty of the world. He found the lines:

"They are unpitied from their birth
　　And homeless in men's sight
Who love, better than the earth,
　　Wild plum at night."

He felt his emptiness, like a dark shadow with substance, weighing down upon his spirit.

∎

Father Fabian Chavez, though not really overweight, waddled when he walked, leading Martine along the path through the books piled to his hips. The kitchen floor was clear, but the counters were filled with many volumes. They took seats at a plain wooden table where Father Fabian poured two glasses of claret.

"Oh, yes, yes, yes," he bubbled, "one day I'm going to gather all these books up, sort them out and make some shelves. You know, I've never given away a book; but I am going to let you choose those you would like to have. I know they would have a good home with you. Some people have no respect for these marvellous respositories of God's and man's knowledge. Once, when I was in high school, I knew a young Japanese man who had such reverence for books that whenever he received a new volume, he would bow to it to show his great respect.

"Books are superior entertainment in every way to television or those awful motion pictures. Those things are empty, so artificial. Have you ever really pondered how truly remarkable it is that millions of human beings, at any given time, will sit for hours mesmerized by light patterns being grouped and regrouped on a screen?"

"I guess when you think about it that way," said an amused Martine, "it is a pretty inane way to spend time. Of course now that you're retired, Father, you can entertain yourself in several ways, like driving to various places."

"Oh, my, my, my, young Father Martine, I don't drive," protested Father Fabian. "I've never even driven a car—such awful smelly things."

"How do you get around?"

"It's no problem. I've always taken public transportation, or occasionally a friend will take pity on me and drive me if I really need to be some place at a specific time. Really, I've walked most of my life here in Santa Fe. How do you think I have lived so long, into my eighties?"

"I have always enjoyed our visits, Father," said Martine gravely, but today I have come on business, or rather to beg your indulgence. I very much need your spiritual help and advice. You must not hesitate to tell me if you feel it is an imposition."

"Goodness, gracious, me," said Father Fabian with a distressed look, "can anything so terrible have happened to you, dear Father Martine? It is never an imposition to share the burden of another human being. Pray tell me whatever it is troubling you so. I shall listen with sympathy.

"Father Fabian, I shall just put this to you in one swift, unvarnished blow," said Martine grimly, as he noted apprehension growing on the old priest's face. "I have committed two grievous mortal sins. I have broken my vow of chastity and I have submitted to and taken pleasure in carnal relations with a person of...my own...sex." Martine lost his voice and breath as he finished the sentence; but there was no look of horror on Father Fabian's face. He only appeared to be saddened.

"I might add," Martine continued. "I have not been to my father-confessor yet. I have put it off because, among other reasons, I wanted to sort things out and know very clearly how I feel before I go into formal confession. Obviously, Father, I have lost the serene life I have always known. My world is disturbed and shaken, and even more shattering is the possibility that I may be gay, something I had not suspected until this encounter. It is humiliating to bring this to you, but I thought you would understand."

"Indeed, indeed. Yes, I understand," said Father Fabian soothingly. "It's not the end of the world, nor the end of your life, or even the end of your work in the priesthood. And if it's any comfort to you, over my long years I have known a number of young priests who fell into similar situations. They recovered, went on to have exemplary lives and careers in the church. There's little our Creator will not forgive, if he is asked with a truly contrite heart. On the other hand, my dear Martine, it's men who sometimes have such awful difficulties with forgiving themselves and others—especially others."

"Where do I begin to sort this out and start putting it right?" asked Martine earnestly.

"You start with contrition, which I am sure you have," Father Fabian said in a low voice. "You go to our Father and the Blessed Virgin with such a weighty matter and they will take pity, have mercy on you and all of this will be swept away, blotted out, forgiven if you are absolutely sincere in saying and believing that it will never happen again. Oh, my, and yes, you will make your confession to the church, ask forgiveness for breaking your vow, and then you will be given penance.

"You, Father Martine, if I know you as I think I do, feel this is the end of your life and work as you have known them. Well, young Sir, do please remember what Christ said to the woman taken in prostitution. He told her to go forth and sin no more. Is one sexual transgression any worse than another? Considering the teachings of Jesus Christ, it would not appear so. All of them are of equal weight and are forgiven equally if the petitioner has a true change of heart. Rest assured, my young friend, contrition and forgiveness do wondrous things. They 'knit up the ravell'd sleeve of care' as Shakespeare was want to say.

"You, as a priest, know all of this; however, right now you need reassurance. You feel alone in the midst of ruin and despair. Remember down deep the miraculous repair that descends from Heaven when we ask for it."

"You make it sound so easy, Father," said Martine with a brighter tone to his voice. "Still there's the thing of my nature. How can I pursue a life of work in the church if I am truly homosexual? That nature would be in conflict with my mission; and, most bitter of all, would be the knowledge that I could never exist again in a true state of grace."

"Oh, dear, dear, dear me!" said Father Fabian, wagging a finger. "Ask, implore, beseech, my dear young man. Ask, and a miracle will change your nature, will quench the fires of passion and allow you to sublimate desire and sexual need in your devotion to the Ancient of Days and to the church. You have the faith. I know that. Yes, yes, yes. It will move this mountain for you."

"You have such optimism, such joy—joyous optimism, Father."

"Well, I'll declare. Of course, young friend. This is what we are about in this sacred fraternity. We must believe, in fact know that this kind of miracle will happen. All of life is a miracle. Wouldn't we be in terrible straits if we didn't believe that life itself will continue? Without such optimism man would be a doomed creature, indeed."

But Martine wondered what he would do if the miracle didn't happen. He decided that to entertain that question would indicate that he, a priest of all people, had a very tenuous grip on his faith. Instead he asked, "Father Fabian, have you ever known a priest who was delivered through the intervention of the Almighty, a miracle as you called it?"

"Heavens yes; yes, yes, yes. This is not something uncommon. Such a priest turns to the most powerful cure in the universe— prayer—asking for intervention in his life."

"And does the miracle take place immediately or over a period of time?"

"Mercy, I just don't know. I don't think the young priest ever told me what came about as a result of his prayers, or how the miracle happened."

Martine wanted to press the point, but thought better of it. Such intense questioning might offend his elderly friend.

"Oh, pray do let me tell you: the thing that's most important in your situation is to be able to forgive yourself, Father Martine. Without that there can be no miracle, no feeling that you have been absolved and no peace of mind. As you freely forgive others and ask God to forgive others be just as magnanimous to yourself."

Father Fabian paused and squinted as he looked at Martine. With a sly smile, he asked, "Have I given you anything of value, some small light that will help illuminate the path for your weary steps?"

As in the conversation with Dalrymple, Martine could not find much solace. Forgiving himself was out of the question until he was convinced that he was forgiven by Heaven and the church. As for asking for a miracle to exorcise the beast that he felt had taken possession, he had been sending up a prayer for deliverance almost every hour since that rainy night. He nodded and smiled weakly at his elderly mentor.

"Father Fabian, as always you have held me spellbound and the evening has vanished. I will remain in your debt for your guidance, understanding and kindness. Thank you so much."

"Gracious, me! It was nothing more than my duty," Father Fabian said as he led Martine toward the door.

∎

Many years earlier, an army commander at Santa Fe, Colonel Edwin Vose Sumner, had looked about him shortly after the territory was seized from Mexico and called it "that sink of vice and extravagance." The extravagance—color, cultures and raw natural beauty— still existed but the Catholic Church for most of the nineteenth century labored diligently to cleanse the vice and produce a land of righteous citizenry. This effort was almost palpable in the archdiocesan office where Martine found himself waiting for his appointment with Monsignor Cipriano Montoya, second in rank only to Archbishop Gallegos.

Montoya was versed in church and cannon law. Priests of the diocese avoided him whenever possible. He was known for his articulate but tart manner and his impeccable dress, even when appearing in the somewhat monotonous church vestments.

Wearing his cassock, he sat at a large mahogany desk, his eyes unsmiling and unblinking behind rimless glasses, as Martine was ushered in. Behind him was a huge window that framed part of the cathedral beyond. He appeared as a dark outline in this window as he, without offering a hand, motioned Martine to a huge leather-covered chair in front of his desk. With its prominent wings at shoulder height, it seemed ready to swallow those who sat in it.

"Regrettably, I have not had as much time as I would like to devote to your pastorate, Father dePaul," he began. "However, your parishioners in general give good report of your stewardship. Are there any difficulties I should know about in the San Luis Rey Parish?"

"Not in the parish, not to my knowledge, Father," replied Martine, aware of his sweating palms. "I have come, as you know, to make my confession."

To Martine's consternation, Father Cipriano said, "There is a great deal on my agenda this day, so I know you won't mind if we keep this simple." He made the sign of the Cross and took from his desk a stole to officiate, kissed it and placed it around his shoulders. Martine's uneasiness grew as he knelt on the small prayer bench at the side of his chair and crossing himself he began: "Bless me father for I have sinned. I have broken my sacred vow of chastity in having had carnal knowledge with someone of my own sex; and I believe that my nature and thoughts have become impure because I still retain a physical attraction for this person."

Father Cipriano insistantly held up his hand. "Father dePaul, since this involves the sanctity of your office as it relates to the church, I feel your confession is not one I can respond to in the proper sacramental and liturgical manner. I am going to ask you to make your confession directly to Archbishop Gallegos. He is the proper authority to deal with a confession of this nature. On a few past occasions young priests have come before me with similar confessions and I have felt constrained to ask that these be brought to the archbishop. He was in complete agreement with my decision.

"Archbishop Gallegos is out of the state on business for several days, or I would arrange an audience immediately. Let me suggest that you call for an appointment at the beginning of the week. In the meantime, I ask that you return to your duties. You are aware, of course, that the degree of an individual priest's sin or righteousness does not detract from or add to the miracle of consecration. Also, I would suggest that you not exacerbate your personal and spiritual status by any repetition of the activity you have just described."

Martine was both relieved and hurt by the monsignor's action. He wanted the matter resolved, ending the suspense of what might be imposed as penance. However he was relieved that Father Cipriano would not be the authority imposing the penance. At his hands, it could be severe without any mitigation.

Martine's anxiety prompted an improper question: "May I ask how those similar cases were disposed of by the diocese?"

"You may not," Father Cipriano replied brusquely. "And now if you will be so kind, you may take your leave."

Driving toward San Carlo, Martine still felt a burning humiliation. He had left himself open for the rebuke by the haughty chancellor. Now he was in limbo until the archbishop's return. What had happened to the precise control he once exercised over his life? Even God had grown silent.

SEVEN

Martine's day had been one of indecision and discord. After celebrating the early morning Mass and saying his final, personal prayers, he had decided to resign, to leave both the parish and the priesthood. But after breakfast and a lengthy discussion with Taegu about the career options open to the youth, Martine wasn't sure. He went back to the church and implored God for some sign. Afterward, as he was standing on the front steps, ready to close the massive door, a sudden gust of wind came from nowhere, seized the thick wooden structure and slammed it shut in his face.

This seemed a direct answer, Martine believed. He had always maintained that most unexplained happenings had logical answers if one dug deeply enough; but the door had been grasped by invisible hands. Nowhere else was there any wind, not a leaf appeared to be moving on any tree in sight. Sorrowfully, he had his answer. It was not one he wanted. On the other hand, why wait for the inevitable, he asked himself. Once free of his commitment, he reasoned, there would be no more conflict between what he believed was his inner person and the teachings and mission of the church.

Martine hurried toward his apartment. At last, thank God, he could see an opening. He could quell the conflict. All was not dark. He opened his fifth beer of the day to help stabilize his resolve, dug out the portable electric typewriter from his college days and composed a letter of resignation:

"As of this date please accept my resignation from the priesthood of the Holy Catholic Church. This also makes effective my resignation as pastor of the Church of San Luis Rey in the Village of San Carlo.

"I ask the forgiveness of God, the Church and yourself, most reverend father, for any consternation or pain my action may cause;

but I can no longer ignore the conflict between my personal life and the mission of the church. Failure to take this action on my part would result in a disservice to both the Church and myself."

After driving to the main post office in Santa Fe and posting his letter, he placed a can of beer in a brown bag and walked toward the Santa Fe River, now only a stream that serves as an oasis of green almost evenly bissecting the old city with grassy banks and groves of cottonwood and spruce trees. This ten-mile long rivulet is fed by pencil-thin tributaries and springs in the Sangre de Cristo Mountains where it rises, trickles through the city and then hurries to the Rio Grande River. This oasis is also a refuge that lures both the loved and the unloved. Sometimes the homeless can find shelter under one of the quaint bridges.

Today, the river park was a respite to Martine who sat down on one of the stone resting places and inspected his surroundings. This was the first time since Cornell days that something was not demanding his attention or waiting to take his time. He was actually seeing grass, trees and sky for the first time in years, he thought. How truly wonderful that the church was no longer about his shoulders. He breathed deeply and decided he would get drunk, falling-down drunk as his student companions used to say at Ithaca.

Martine lay down on the grass, allowing the sun to possess him. He would not have to worry about the chancellor or the archbishop any more. How odd, he thought, that a small piece of paper could change one's whole world within minutes from grief to peace of mind. He reflected on what might have happened if Father Cipriano had allowed the confession to continue and had asked the fatal question: "Are you still physically attracted to this man, this boy?" Deep down he knew he was not free of Lance. This mildly disturbed him as he drifted into sleep, lured by the warmth and his newly unburdened mind. Dimly, he heard a church bell as the world faded.

"Martine, Martine! Wake up. What are you doing here?" He felt a soft hand shaking his shoulder as he came from out of a deep slumber, breathed deeply of the sweet air and opened his eyes to find long tresses and a beautiful face just above his. "Martine, why in the world are you sleeping here with the bums?" asked Cindi.

He studied her face before answering. Lovely, he thought. "I must have fallen asleep," Martine said, sitting up and reaching for his beer that had turned tepid while he slept. "I didn't intend to fall asleep. I was just relaxing, enjoying the out-of-doors and trying to think about some things."

"And did you think them through?" asked Cindy with a smile.

"I guess I did," he said, and then he asked, "Where's Lance?"

"Lance?" she said quizzically. "Why should I know where he is, that loco boy? In Albuquerque, I suppose."

"What's he doing there?"

"Didn't you know?" she asked. "He moved back to his apartment because school is about to start. Didn't he say goodbye? I guess he didn't. I think he was not so much in love with you when he left? You know what I mean. Sometimes I say the wrong word in English. He was not so much your friend anymore. What happened between you two?"

"I don't know," said Martine, a distance coming in his voice. "We had different interests, I guess."

"Anyway, let's not talk about him. This is my big day when I find a beautiful hunk like you sleeping in the park. Better you should sleep some place else like in my bed. But, oh, I forgot. You are married, no?"

Martine paused for a moment, then slowly tilted his head toward Cindi. A large smile spread over his face as he spoke. "You know what? I guess I'm not married anymore, at that."

"Ah, you get a divorce, pretty boy?" she said as her long, carefully manicured fingers ran through his short-cropped black hair. "I think hair like this is so sexy. It turns me on. It is mucho macho." The air tinkled with the sounds of thin silver bracelets on her moving arms.

Martine felt a tinge of excitement as she played with his hair. Shadows were falling on the park and the air was cooler. "Tell you what," he said. "Let's go, and I'll buy you one. I'll follow your car to Los Dos Tortugas."

"Oh, no you won't," she laughed. I left my car at home. I'm walking. I live just over there," and she pointed to an apartment building across the river."

"Okay, we'll go in my car; but we have to walk over and pick it up near the post office." Cindi's fingers caught his hand as they left the river bank.

■

The weather was changing rapidly as they reached the lounge parking lot. Clouds were racing down from the mountains as darkness gathered and a few raindrops were splattering Martine's windshield. Inside, the lounge was warm and cheerful. Everyone seemed to know Cindi as greetings came from all directions. A male voice called out, "Where did you catch that one, Cindi?"

"At the river," she answered, laughing.

Martine ordered three beers, two for himself, and drank the first straight down. He felt an intense thirst, coupled with a desire to celebrate. For the first time in years he didn't have a care in the world.

"Chugalug!" cried Cindi as Martine placed the empty mug firmly on the table. "You drink like a fish. What are you celebrating?"

"Freedom," Martine said with a now-natural wide smile as he began the second mug. "I had forgotten what it felt like not to have a cloud hanging over my head."

"Was she really that bad?" asked Cindi seriously.

"No, actually she was wonderful," said Martine, thinking of the church he turned his back on only hours earlier. "I was the bad one." He held three fingers up toward the bar.

"Hey, Martine! Muchacho!" Cindi exclaimed. "Where are you putting all that booze?"

"In my empty heart."

"Let Cindi fill your heart, let her fill all of you and it will be so good for both of us." Martine felt the warmth of her arm around his back and the touch of her finger tips as they curled around his chest and teased his nipple. He held her free hand tightly and when her warm, wet lips lightly kissed his ear a sudden arousal astonished him. There was no longer a vow to hold him back, repress his desire. The priest was not here to forbid indulgence. His choice was instant and without thinking. He would give in to this lust, something he had never known. Perhaps this was why he had gone wrong in the first place, he reasoned. Now was the opportunity to find the truth, prove his maleness, his virility. The old restraints of the priesthood slipped away without a second thought.

"You never did tell me," Cindi said. "Where are you from and what do you do?

Martine skirted a lie. "I live outside Santa Fe, and I don't do anything—at least not now." He empted his last mug and ordered fresh ones. The alcohol was powering his desire for the woman beside him; and she fueled the drive by allowing his hands to gently explore the exquisite contours of her body.

"It's no wonder, then," she said, "that you are so sexy. If you don't have a job, you have all day to store up all that sexual energy."

"What do you see in me, anyway?" he asked. "I'm not as handsome as Lance. I'm not tall, and I'm certainly not the big, rugged western type."

"You are prettier and sexier. You have machismo. That's something more than just being a stud. You are tall enough—built to make love. I can feel it radiate from you like electricity. I know about these things," she said, moving her fingers over his face, as if she were feeling rather than seeing his good looks. "But still, there is one thing I have not had." She paused.

"What is that?" he asked.

"I have not tasted that glorious mouth."

"Nor I yours," Martine said as he bent his mouth to hers. No one in the crowded lounge noticed as they drank deeply from one another for the first time. This added to Martine's intoxication and made him impervious to the world around them. He no longer cared if anyone knew or guessed who he was.

"Come," she whispered. "The time is right." Martine reached into his jeans and fumbled out a handful of bills. He was unsteady on his feet, but Cindi braced tightly against him so his intoxicated gait would not be noticed. Once outside, he was invigorated by the cool air, but she took his keys and drove.

Inside the tastefully furnished apartment, their clothes began to disappear as they moved toward her bedroom. Martine, more alert now, skinned off his light pullover, leaving his well toned upper torso bare. Beside her bed their mouths met tightly as did their bodies, and Martine's hands peeled away her remaining upper garments, baring breasts for his mouth that moved down her neck greedily toward each nipple. His hands reached for the top snap of his jeans but her hands stopped him.

"No, no, Martine," she said. "You have finally brought this beautiful gift to me, now let me unwrap it." Her deft fingers released him with a light tug and the jeans dropped from his hips. He had never in his adult life had a woman see him naked, he thought, but now he relished the feeling. He was overwhelmed with the thought that it was all part of his maleness, his strength. With a slight pull, his final garment fell away, and Cindi pulled him over her as she eased back on the bed.

"Take me, possess me completely!" she cried as she wrapped her legs around his hairy thighs and their bodies locked, slowly, inexorably together. His unaided entry was pure animal instinct, something he felt they both had lived for all their lives. They moaned as unadulterated sexual pleasure possessed them and soared their bodies toward climax.

"Martine could not stifle his voice as it cried out, "This is it...augh!...augh! Yes, yes!" A tantalizing sensation started deep in his belly and welled up out of him in an eruption of pure ecstasy. Its power gathered Cindi up and as she gave way her cries seemed to cut off her breath that came in bursts. Torn by the joy exacted of her body, she clung to Martine, leaving fingernail marks deep in the flesh of his back. At last it was if they fell into one another and lay still on a plain of placid contentment. Not even a shadow of his previous life's commitment passed across Martine's mind.

He was the first to stir, pulling away and climbing from the bed. He stumbled in the semi-dark room, searching for his jeans and the cigarettes he had bought at Los Dos Tortugas. Cindi turned on her side, her dark eyes quietly watching him. He returned and proped a pillow behind himself, then lit two cigarettes—for himself and Cindi. His eyes gleamed in the flare of the match, his face radiant in the moment before the flare was extinguished.

"God, you're beautiful," she said with finality.

"And so are you," he said as he reached over and cupped her perfect breast. He stared at the outline of her face. It was the classic beauty of Spain, he thought.

"We had no protection," he said, in an emotionless voice.

"I know," she answered. "I loved it."

"But you've just mated with me," Martine said. "I pumped my semen, my seed into your body. What if I impregnated you?"

Cindi sat up laughing. "And I want you to do it again and again and plant your baby in me. I want it so much. I've never wanted that from any man before."

Martine thought what an irony it would be if she became pregnant by him, rather than Lance, the fabled stud. "Why do you want that from me?" he asked. Once again, he could feel the swelling of arousal.

"Because you are the kind of man I want," she said emphatically.

"Damn, there he goes again," Martine said. Being crude and animal was something new to him and he liked it.

"And, damn, here he comes again," said Cindi as she reached for Martine.

A gray dawn had come up over Santa Fe and brushed against the bedroom window when Martine, exhausted, ceased his love making and fell asleep. When he later awakened the room was flooded with daylight and it was close to noon. Cindi was gone. His head ached violently, but he reached to the bedside table without looking and let his hand scramble about for the cigarettes. He lit one and as he smoked it realized he was still totally nude. He liked the sensation. As he thought about the previous evening, he remarked to himself that he had unveiled yet another nature that—sexually at least—was crude, animal, crass, graphic, earthy. His head hurt and he couldn't think; but he was getting aroused and wished Cindi was with him.

Martine stumbled out of bed, found the kitchen and drank several glasses of cold water. He searched the refrigerator for juice. Finding only V-8, he drank it and stood at the window as he smoked another cigarette. He smiled as he thought about Lance. He now understood the sexually driven side of the youth's nature. He realized that he still missed Lance, wanted him in his life. How could this be, he thought. He had abandoned himself totally in his desire for Cindi, but the other part of his nature had not diminished. His spirits fell. Down below on the sidewalk people were looking up at him and pointing when he suddenly realized he was standing before the window nude, in full-blown desire. He moved away, opened a beer, got into bed and drank it and was soon sound asleep. He did not awaken until he felt Cindi's nude body beside him. It was getting dark outside.

Cindi had brought home more beer and as they made love a second night, Martine got totally inebriated once again. When he awakened the next day, Cindi was again gone, but this time his head was really splitting. He went to the refrigerator and opened another beer. It was starting all over again, he thought. He then remembered this was the third day and he had not shaved or showered, or had any clothes on for the entire time.

Fortunately, he thought in the shower, he had called Taegu and asked him to put a note on the church door saying that the priest was indisposed. This thought caused him to smile. He believed that by now the archdiocesan office had received his letter and probably had called someone to temporary duty at San Luis Rey. He toweled off and threw the towel aside. In the kitchen he found crackers, opened more beer and lay back on the bed to wait for Cindi. All he wanted was to continue mating with Cindi, even give her the baby she wanted.

That night in bed he told her, "I've got to go home tomorrow. No kidding."

"You can never go home again," Cindi purred. "You are my love slave. I am going to keep you in my bed forever."

"Okay," he said. "I've got to get a change of clothes and a few things like my shaving kit, and I'll be back. I haven't had a stitch of clothing on in four days."

"I like you better without clothes," she laughed. "Don't put them on ever again."

"Hey, I can't go around town in the buff," exclaimed Martine.

"Wear a...what do you call it?...a fig leaf. I'll buy you one, a big one."

∎

It was good to be outside, Martine thought as he drove to San Carlo. He hadn't been out of Cindi's apartment for days. He was already on his third beer of the morning. Drinking had become a way of life after he found it soothed his aching head in the morning, helped him not to think or care about his lost career, as he had taken to calling it, and the most important thing of all, it powered his incredible sex drive. Even as he was driving he wanted to take his clothes off.

At the studio he leafed briskly through his mail, keeping only the letter from his mother. Then he remembered he should take his typewriter back to Cindi's apartment. He decided he would start typing his letters home, getting some practice on the keyboard. Perhaps he would go into public relations or something. He filled a bag with several pairs of faded jeans, a couple of pull-overs and the few white shirts that had been laundered. After opening another beer, he decided to drive to Los Dos Tortugas and maybe spend part of the afternoon playing shuffleboard.

He looked around the apartment a last time and spotted one of his clerical collars on the mantelpiece. It was a reminder of who he once was. He smiled ruefully as he picked it up. That's all he had left of a whole life: his work as a priest, his years in seminary and finally this, he told himself. How odd that such a little bit remained, he thought; but then there wasn't much material baggage when dealing with things of the spirit. It was all gone but this, he whispered, and with it Lance. What a hell of a thing you did to me, Lance, he said aloud as he locked the apartment door.

∎

It was a rare afternoon for Martine. He reached a level of intoxication and after that no matter how much he drank it seemed to have no effect. He simply felt more elated. In this frame of mind he didn't think of his past life, as he called it sometimes. But, he did think again and again how wonderful it was to be free. He reveled in it, savored it. He could go anywhere, do anything and who was to tell him there was a rule that said he could not? He loved all the things he had found in his new life. He couldn't believe there had been a rule keeping them away, barring him. The church, Lance— all that—were distant shadows he might never look at again.

Suddenly, he felt a hand on his shoulder and looked up to find Old Bonnie showing her toothless smile and standing just behind him. "Look," he said, "I'm in no mood for insults, so just move it along elsewhere!"

"Naw, naw, Old Bonnie'll be good," she assured him as she skittered bent and crab-like into the booth. I want to tell you a story," she soothed, looking up from under the brim of her hat.

"What kind of story?" Martine asked skeptically. "I thought you were a painter, not a story teller."

"I am a painter," she hissed, "the best in these hills. I paint what others cannot see. They can only paint the obvious. What good is that, when anyone can go see whatever it is for themselves? But I also tell stories, true stories that only I know. Let me smoke a cigarette and buy me a beer and I'll tell you."

Martine held two fingers up toward the bar and looked back at the gnarled old woman. "What is this story about, Bonnie."

"It's about you?"

"What?" he said incredulously. "How do you know anything about me?"

"Old Bonnie knows these things. She learned from Indians years ago when she was their daughter."

"You're an Indian?"

"I didn't say that," she said, making her hissed words more emphatic. "I said I was their daughter, grew up with them when no one else would have me."

"Why do you want to tell me this?"

"Because if I don't, the spirits will give me no peace. The only way I can lay them to rest is by repeating what they tell me. Are you ready to listen?" She blew acrid cigarette smoke in his direction as he sat quietly.

"You do not belong here. You were sent by the Great One into this world to do good things for other people. You make them happy when they see you, and they smile. You bring cheer to them and with this comes hope that they themselves can make things better for the world around them. Without you knowing it or without them knowing it, you give them hope. That's why you were sent among us."

Martine was uncomfortable and he remembered with a shudder that she was called La Bruja.

"But you have lost your way. The devil came and slept with you and turned you in a different direction, away from the Great One and what he sent you here to do. You have found the flesh and lust and you have turned your back on your work and this is obstructing your path back to the Great One and it has made him full of sorrow."

"What are you talking about?" asked a bewildered Martine, but knowing in his mind that the old woman was hitting a nerve with every word.

Her hiss grew louder. "You are a priest. Your work is with the spirit and things unseen."

"What does all this nonsense mean?" Martine demanded.

"I don't know," Old Bonnie answered him. "This was what the spirits told me."

"Who are these spirits?" he was asking when he was interrupted by a sudden commotion behind him. Cindi had arrived in an explosion of laughter and conversation with several friends in the lounge.

Martine turned back to find the old woman had vanished without making a sound. He shivered as Cindi placed her warm moist lips against his.

"So, I find you at last?" she questioned. "Buy me a drink."

"I just had the strangest experience," he said. "Old Bonnie was here telling me some weird tale about what the spirits had told her about me.

"Ah, that's La Bruja," said Cindi, dismissing it with a wave of her hand. "She talks crazy."

"But she was here and when I looked away she just disappeared."

"Forget about it, Muchacho. She is just a loco old lady. Everybody in Santa Fe knows that. I have fantastico news for you." she said, nuzzling him. "I am carrying your baby, little Martine."

"Aw, Cindy," he laughed. "It's only been a week. You couldn't know a thing like that yet. How could you?"

"I just know," she twinkled. "I have this good feeling like part of you inside me, and I know what it is. A little muchacho inside me, growing. It makes me very wild with happiness. Does that make you happy?"

"Of course, I would be happy to know we had made a child," he smiled. "But don't you think we ought to wait until we know for sure. We're not even married yet?

"Hey, who says we have to get married to have a wonderful baby?"

"Look," Martine said. "There's a more practical matter we need to think about right now. I'll be sharing your place and you're not paying for it by yourself," he said decisively, taking a checkbook from his pocket.

"It's nada," Cindi laughed. "You pay me for it every night."

"You take this," he said, handing her a check, "and I'll give you one every month."

"Holy Moses," she almost shouted in amazement. "This is a thousand dollars and it's on a bank in New York. Muchacho, where did you get money like this?"

"Have you forgotten I had a job?" he asked.

"More like a gold mine than a job. What do you really do, Martine?"

"Sort of like teaching," he dodged. "You know, you ask all these questions, but I don't know what you do every day."

"I'm a nurse at the hospital," she replied.

"That's just what I need every morning," Martine said with a laugh as he put a hand to his head.

∎

Martine's euphoria over being free did not last long. He was now spending most of his days drinking, sometimes in Santa fe, or at other times he would drive to Taos or Espanola. He would get back in time to be with Cindi at night.

One morning, he awakened with an extremely vicious hang-over and reached for his customary medication. This particular morning as he drank the beer to quiet the pain in his head, he could not keep thoughts and anxiety about his life from crowding into his mind. He had not wanted to admit it, but his new-found freedom was nothing more than a vacuum. In it he was indulging his body and his senses day after day, and when he took stock of these things they were leading him nowhere. He hadn't made a single effort to find a job that could use his abilities, and when he thought about it there was nothing in the secular world that interested him.

The story the old lady unfolded still haunted him, and it made him remember how concerned he once was about the world and how he had believed that if men really lived by their inner spirit and its dictates then eventually human fear, pain and misery could be eliminated forever. Why had he just thrown it all to the four winds and given himself up to a life of carnality? He had discovered a flawed nature and concluded that he was unworthy to carry forth the church's mission. He had thought this latest preoccupation would be the perfect instrument to erase the first flaw. It hadn't worked. Now he had two flaws, he reasoned.

There was nothing to offer him a clue—only the endless days and nights of self-inflicted depravity. Was this really freedom, he asked himself. He knew deep inside he was still a Catholic. But, this present life was producing sin, while his previous life was oriented toward creating good.

Martine got out of bed and dressed. He had to find answers, but the more he thought about his life, the more questions arose. All the people he had sought out for spiritual help and advice had turned out to be Job's Comforters, leaving him only with weak and untenable answers. He was convinced that only he could provide the answers. He spent what was left of the day in the apartment examining his situation, but in the end he felt more depressed than when he started.

Cindi came home in an ugly mood.

"You did not tell Cindi the truth," she sputtered machine gun-like. "You lied to her. You made a fool of her."

"Whoa, wait," he protested. "What are you talking about? I may have lots of faults but I try not to lie."

"You lied to me about who you are." Her eyes flashed fire. "I met someone today from San Carlo and she knows you. She knows you as the priest at the San Carlo church."

"I was the priest at San Luis Rey Church in San Carlo," he said patiently. "I resigned and left the priesthood. There was no point in telling you all that."

"No, but you said you were married and that you had gotten a divorce and all those lies."

"There was no lie there. As a priest, I was married to the church. When I left, I divorced the church.

"You told me you were a teacher. Where did you get all that money? Priests don't make big bucks like that," she cried, shaking her finger at him.

"Look, Cindi," he said, remaining calm. "A priest does teach. As for the money, my father gave me an endowment years ago, and if I need money for something extra, I draw on that. Does that answer your questions?"

"But a long time ago you let Lance say you were married!"

"And indeed I was," said Martine slowly.

Tears were beginning to run down her face. "Oh, this is so bad for Cindi. I have made love to a priest. I am in terrible trouble. That is something you should never do."

Martine reached out and held her struggling body close. "I am no longer a priest. Listen to me. I resigned nearly two weeks ago. You're not going to have any trouble."

"I know," she sobbed, "but it is bad luck to sleep with a priest or bishop, and what about our baby? A priest's baby!"

"It's not a priest's baby! Hey, we don't even know if you are pregnant; and even if you were, I was not a priest at the time.

Besides lots of priests, even cardinals and popes, have had children. Some of them famous."

"I don't feel right about it," said Cindi, calming down. "I will have to think about it. Anyway, you sleep on the sofa tonight."

"Aw, Cindi, that sofa's too short and besides it's hard. Tell you what. I will sleep on my side of the bed and you sleep on yours."

"What if something happens in the bed?" she asked.

"Nothing is going to happen," Martine assured her. "You know, if we are going to live together, you'll have to get over this."

This was a complication Martine had not anticipated. He would untie the knots tomorrow, perhaps drive up to Espanola and enjoy the countryside. There was a quaint little bar he knew about up that way.

EIGHT

As he awakened Martine experienced his worst hangover ever. He wished he had not spent the previous afternoon drinking in Espanola and then finally at Los Dos Tortugas. suddenly he remembered the note that Taegu had left him at the lounge, and he glanced over to see the wrinkled paper on the bedside table, reassuring him that it was not a dream that the archbishop was seeking a conference with him. He once more opened the note, worn from being in his back pocket and strained to make out the words. The content left no doubt: he was asked to make an appointment with Archbishop Gallegos.

He had assumed that the only communication from the church would be a letter accepting his resignation, or one that just plain booted him out. This was a turn he had not anticipated and the thought of it made him uneasy. What could the archbishop want? What more was there to say? But, suddenly, his spirits were lifted by the prospect of a face-to-face encounter. Perhaps it would help clear his mind and focus on the direction he needed to follow. He knew he could not go on drinking and wasting his time.

But the most pressing problem right now was his head and queasy stomach. Perhaps a shower, juice and a few aspirin would get him jump-started. Without getting out of bed, he telephoned the office of the archdiocese and after a short wait was connected to the archbishop's secretary. Yes, Archbishop Gallegos wanted to see Father dePaul at two this afternoon. That was a relief. He still had a few hours to undo the effects of the alcohol. Then he suddenly remembered what the secretary had said. She had called him Father dePaul. Father? That meant his resignation had not been accepted.

How could he tell Cindi if that was the case. But, as far as he was concerned, he was no longer a member of the priesthood.

The steaming shower helped, but it could not erase the feeling that he was back into his old problems again, that there seemed to be no freedom for him anywhere he sought it. As the hot water poured over him, he asked God over and over how he had gotten to this point.

■

Martine paused in the shadow of the great cathedral, its immensity dominating the city around it. Its creator, Archbishop Jean Baptist Lamy, intended it to be that way— so much so that it had to be built around another church, the Parroquia, because that was the location Lamy wanted. The cornerstone was laid October 10, 1869, but the archbishop would not live out the quarter century and more that it took to carve his dream stone by stone and rear it up to the glory of God.

But, it was more than a dream that built this romanesque monument of the archdiocese. It took miracles to overcome the obstacles. There was never enough money because of financial panics that swept the country time and again; the stone cutters from Italy and France constantly ran out of stone; and a railroad strike cut off supplies to the frontier at one time. And if these were not enough, the architect, Frenchman Francoise Mallet was shot and killed by the archbishop's nephew because of attentions Mallet supposedly paid the young man's wife. The nephew was acquitted. The vast cathedral, one hundred and twenty feet long and with towers eighty feet high, was finally consecrated October 18, 1895.

Martine entered the cathedral's cool dark world. He had time for a short supplication before his appointment with Archbishop Gallegos. It seemed eons since Martine had been in the presence of God, and he felt like an unwelcome intruder in the hallowed environs. He knelt at the high altar.

"Oh, God, remember not my offenses for they are many in Thy sight. I detest all my sins and I am deeply sorry for them and I offer my life as propitiation for having offended Thee, if that is accepable. I beseech Thee, Oh Lord, to lead me in the direction that pleases Thee. In the name of Jesus Christ, Thy Son, who came into the world to save sinners."

Archbishop Gallegos, wearing his collar and dressed in a black suit, came from behind his desk, smiled and shook Martine's hand. The prelate's pectoral cross was large and black, as if carved from a piece of coal. His hands were those of a workman, large and rough.

"Martine, if I may take the liberty of calling you that," the archbishop said jovially, "I feel remiss in many ways for having visited with you only twice since you came into the archdiocese and took over as the pastor of San Luis Rey Church. I do have a defense, though. I have heard nothing but glowing reports about you since you picked up the shepherd's staff at San Carlo. Knowing this, I could see no reason to tinker. What is it they say, 'Don't try to fix that which is working.' In many ways that's how I view the hard-working priests of my domain.

"Obviously I did not call you here to make your priestly confession because such a requirement is rather after the fact in view of your resignation. And, Martine, let me stress here that you are still a priest until you have been officially released by the church. It's like getting a discharge from the Army, only we don't have any court-martial authority," he added with a slight smile.

Martine's knuckles whitened as he gripped the arms of his chair. "Archbishop, if I may interrupt," he said. "I was of the firm belief that I had automatically removed myself from the priesthood by the unconscionable breaking of the vows of my office and by my stated resignation to this archdiocese."

"Well, of course, you can adopt any individual status you wish in your own mind," the archbishop said. "We have no authority over that; but as I said, you are a priest in the church's view until such time as the Vatican issues you an official release. So what are you thinking about now, Martine?"

"I think my life is in chaos," said Martine. "Coming here from the almost cloistered life of the seminary, I found great happiness in my service to God and to the church at San Carlo. It was what I had always wanted—with passion, I might add; and I guess right there was the beginning of grievious error, the sin of pleasing myself through acquiring what I wanted, rather than what God wanted.

"Then when sin knocked at my door, I opened it and became the willing host, breaking my sacred vow of chastity...."

"Let me interrupt," said the archbishop with a kindly smile, "What is this terrible sin you have committed. I know that this is not a confession in the liturgical sense, but it might help if we could clarify some points."

"I was a willing participant in sexual lust with someone of my own sex. If there is any shred of defense at all, I can say that he was the aggressor. As a result I discovered I had a physical attraction for this man, and I view this as making me unfit for service to God and the church."

"Oh, I sense an awful lot of self-condemnation here, Father Martine," the archbishop said gravely. "A broken vow can be repaired with a broken and contrite heart and with absolution and penance, as, indeed, can all sins of the flesh. However, it is this so-called discovery that bothers me. Is this why you resigned?" from the priesthood?"

Martine noticed how puzzled the archbishop looked, furrows spreading across his brow. He came from behind his desk and sat in front of Martine.

"In large part, yes," said Martine. "I had come to the conclusion that I was gay. I felt I had fallen from grace, could never achieve it again."

"If you were released from the priesthood," the archbishop asked, "is this the lifestyle you would pursue?"

"No, it is not. But then, I do not think that a person with this orientation is worthy to wear the collar."

"Martine, none of us is worthy," said the archbishop quietly. "We are all tempted by one sin or another. Almost all of us struggle against the sins that lurk in thought, word or deed. I think Thomas a` Kempis said it perfectly:

"'There is no man wholly free from temptation so long as he liveth, because we have the root of temptation within ourselves, in that we are born in concupiscence. One temptation or sorrow passeth, and another cometh; and always we shall have somewhat to suffer, for we have fallen from perfect happiness.'"

"Do you remember that?"

"Indeed I do, archbishop.

"Martine, as a priest of the church you knew that none of these offenses placed a man and a priest beyond redemption. You knew that through proper attitude on your part you could be absolved by the church. I think the problem here is that you cannot forgive yourself. I know from your record and past history you were an extremely devout person. Now you cannot accept that you have fallen.

"Whether you stay in the church or leave, I want you to begin working at forgiving yourself. But, Martine, more than this, I want to reclaim you for the church. This is why I still have this in my coat pocket." He reached inside his coat and pulled out Martine's letter of resignation. "I have not acted on this and would not do so without finding the burr under your saddle, as they say here in the West."

Suddenly, a clock behind Martine chimed three times. The archbishop looked at his watch, then turned to Martine. "This is my afternoon for fresh air. I could take you with me. I have a special place I go to in the mountains. Are you willing?"

When Martine looked hesitant, Archbishop Gallegos said, "My driver will take us. There's a special lookout about midway up to the timberline that I find peaceful. It isn't far from the ski basin."

In the outer office, the archbishop told his secretary he was leaving for the day, reached for a silver-headed cane and led Martine to a side exit where a vintage Cadillac and a driver were waiting. Once inside and the car had pulled away, the archbishop asked: "Do you want to leave the church, Martine?"

"When I wrote the letter, I really did," he replied. "When I thought I was free, it was like having all the cares of the world lifted. I was truly free...I felt no longer burdened. Now, after several weeks of indulging in every whim and passion that I fancy, I realize I am more in bondage than ever."

The archbishop raised his eyebrows and there was a twinkle in his eyes as he said, "So you've discovered we can't really be free, have you? Our freedoms are found within our disciplines, whatever ones we choose—a life of dedication or one of indulgence."

"Martine," the archbishop continued, adopting a confidential tone, "I'm going to get into an area where church superiors should tread lightly, but I feel you're a special case. I know a great deal about your past."

When he saw Martine's bewildered look, he explained quickly, "Oh, yes, Pat Monahan, his imminence, the cardinal, and I are old classmates and we have spoken often about you. From all he and I both know, we believe you have a spirit blessed with grace, the very sort of individual the church needs most. I know you may feel that what you are experiencing is a fall from grace, but that is not a permanent state."

As the car climbed into the mountains and Martine thought about what the archbishop was saying, he suddenly remembered the old woman's words: he had been sent into the world to bring about good in the lives of others. He wondered what Cindi would make of all this.

"You can park along here anywhere," Archbishop Gallegos told his driver, and turning to Martine, "Our spot is just down that path." He pointed to a worn footpath. They followed the little trail through towering pine trees for about a hundred yards where it opened out into a natural stone amphitheater, the stage of which was the whole Rio Grande Valley. "Take a seat," said the archbishop, "and see what God hath wrought." The vastness almost took Martine's breath. He was glad to be here, he thought, and happy to be sober for the first time in days.

"We have a lot of things to talk about," said the archbishop, pulling a shawl about his shoulders against the chill in the air at this higher altitude. "First, I think it is important to let you know what I think about the transgression you have related. I think it is abominable. Are there others?"

"Yes, archbishop, there are. I have been living with a woman and have experienced almost unending sexual relations with her. Further, I have wasted my time and talent in days and nights of drunkenness."

Not even the faintest hint of dismay or disapproval crossed the archbishop's face. "Young Father Martine, it seems to me you have opened the gates of lust and allowed the flood to sweep you away. The church has forgiven greater sins and many of its saints had pasts that made the angels blush. Saint Augustine, before he repented, lived in sin with a woman and fathered her child. In fact, he was even guilty of a heresy against the faith at one point in his life when he was in league with the Manichaeans. Our own Saint Francis, before his repentance, pursued a life of wine, women and song; and Paul of Tarsus began his career as an enemy and persecutor of the church. If your heart sincerely changes, then you will be able, in time, to leave these sins of commission behind you. That's what repentance and forgiveness are all about, as you well know."

"But, archbishop, what about this first relationship and what it may indicate about my nature?" Martine asked with a frown.

"That you may be gay—a homosexual?" Martine nodded gravely.

"First, if you have been sinning with a woman continuously, then certainly you have misclassified yourself, but let's say for the sake of argument that you are correct, that you are gay. What could you do about it? You were born that way, if that is the case. Scientists now believe it is a condition—an orientation if you will—that is in a gene that only women can pass to their children.

"Such a one is a creature of God like the rest of us. If that person chooses to go against church teaching, leading a life of lust and depravity, then we know that this is sin, do we not?"

Martine amazed himself by holding up a finger of protest to interrupt the archbishop. "But how can it be that God permits the creation of people with such natures? That defies all logic in theology and in what I know of morality. If such individuals follow their natures and experience pleasure, then is it not a sin? This certainly is not true in the case of the married heterosexuals? How is this fair, archbishop?"

"You question God, Father Martine? Do you remember when Job questioned God's will, what the Almighty told him? He said to Job, in effect, that God is God and you are puny man. I might paraphrase those lines from Job and ask you where you were when God created the universe and the morning stars all sang together?

"I cannot tell you why such natures appear in human beings, Martine. There are some questions in our world that have no answer. Remember we live in an age where scientific inquiry has conditioned us to believe that if there is a question there is also an answer. But this is not necessarily so. You see here just such a question. However, as I said, these people are no less God's creatures than the rest of us. They just seem to have an extra burden to bear in our intolerant world. If they adhere devoutly to the church's teachings, they may not indulge in sexual pleasures, or lusts; but then neither may we, the members of the priesthood. Neither can any Catholic who would live free of sin in the sight of God. Is that a burden, Father Martine—a Cross to bear? It should not be. This is the thing Christ has asked his servants to do.

"Martine, I want you to remain a servant of God and the church. I'll not let you falter or detour. I will do all in my power, personally, to have you remain. It would be a grave mistake to let you go without a struggle. It might even be an offense against Heaven."

Martine turned with astonishment to the Archbishop: "Whatever do you mean, archbishop?"

Archbishop Gallegos looked out over the vast river valley and chose his words carefully. "You, Martine, may, just may, have been especially sent from God. I know from your past history that you were a boy and a man with special grace, special goodness and people were moved by your example. In times of human crisis, God has picked reluctant and sometimes even sinful men to do his will in this world."

Martine remembered again the words of the old woman. How very strange, he thought, that here, once again, was the same idea. Instead of God she had used the words, the Great One and said it was this being who had sent him into the world. Who am I, indeed, he wondered.

"God has never spoken to me," Martine said almost apologetically. I am no Joan of Arc or Moses. I am having a hard time concentrating on His will just in my personal life."

"Ah," said the archbishop, waving his open hand from side to side in contradiction, "God has spoken to you in giving you an extra measure of blessedness, a shot in the spirit, if you will. Don't you think He intends you to use this gift in serving Him?

"Men have debated endlessly about the purpose on this blue-green sphere floating through all time in the limitless space of the universe. I think we in the church know, do we not? We are here to serve others, sacrificing our lives, ambitions and desires in the process. Some of us never find the place to serve. Others, like the priests and friars who came out here hundreds of years ago, gave their careers, their health and often their lives in martyrdom to build a church in an alien and hostile land. Do you know that at one time— in the revolt of 1680—twenty-one priests were massacred by some of the rebellious people?

"We live today in an alien and hostile world that by its cruelty, indifference and venality makes the past look like Eden. There is a crisis of spirit of such proportions as to be inconceivable. People by the millions are indifferent to their own kind, the hunger, the misery and the suffering. They are indifferent to the greed and selfishness that is destroying the earth on which they live. They are heedless that their own deeds cause pain and death. The very fabric of society is fraying.

"As I see it, we don't have a lot of time left to redeem mankind. So why shouldn't I and others who know you, Martine, want to believe that the church needs soldiers like yourself. It means sacrifice on your part and for those who join you. But we are truly redeemed through sacrifice of our lives. Sacrifice is the highest purpose of the individual human being. Ah, that I were younger and could join the fight in that way again."

Martine had turned his back to survey the valley below. "Will you come back and pick up the sword, Father Martine?" The archbishop tapped the rock beside him with his cane for emphasis.

"I want to come back, archbishop," he replied earnestly as he turned and faced the prelate. "But I want to make certain this time that I will not be diverted from my course by this weak flesh, this vacillating will, this fragile body."

"Martine, one cannot always completely bend their nature to their will, and sometimes they may never achieve the perfection they seek," said the archbishop gently.

"Forgive me, archbishop, for not making myself clear," said Martine. "I should have said that I must be able to have my spirit guide me in my work. I think John revealed this truth perfectly when he said that 'God is a spirit and they that worship Him must worship Him in spirit and in truth.'"

"And when will you know if you are ready to come back?" the archbishop asked.

"I will have reached a decision by tomorrow," Martine answered.

"Excellent! I shouldn't like the suspense to endure beyond that."

Martine edged toward the rim of the cliff for a better look at the Rio Grande, the mountains beyond and the valley floor. He could see San Carlo and the Three-J Ranch in the distance. He thought of Lance and in his mind he could see a laughing boy, his wild hair filled with sunlight and his vigorous body radiating an appetite for life, riding his horse into the shining hills forever. Lance, pagan and free of constraint, would remain imprisoned in Martine's memory like some summer butterfly sealed in a solid crystal cube. But this memory was all that would remain. Martine suddenly realized he was unfettered, free.

A quiet and gray sobriety swept over him as in a landscape claimed by silence after the fury of the storm is spent. Martine knew he would begin to rediscover himself, find vestiges of his own, once-joyous life, little odds and ends of his shattered past. He would set about the task of putting them back together. Out of the reconstruction would come a new life very unlike the old innocent one. It would be given definition by his sense of mission and duty within the disciplines of his faith and of the church.

Martine's realization was interrupted by the archbishop's voice rising above the loud whispers of the wind in the pines. "I have something I think you will want back," he said, removing the envelope from his coat. He handed it to Martine. "If you should decide not to return to us, drop this back in the mail slot at my office tomorrow before five in the afternoon. Then we will regretfully execute the final documents to free you from the church. I hope I shall never see this envelope again."

The sun had turned its face away from the mountain's upper reaches and shadows were now gathering in the ranks of pine as Martine and Archbishop Gallegos walked toward the car.

"Martine, there is one more thing that I think you will understand. While this has not been a confession, I shall bless you nonetheless and impose a penance on you. I want you to resign as the priest of San Luis Rey. I want you to start over in another place. I'm sure you know that this was to have been only a provisional assignment for you. His Eminence, the cardinal, arranged it so that if you felt it was not working out, you could return to New York after one year. That year is up."

"I understand completely," said Martine.

■

Night had settled over Santa Fe by the time Archbishop Gallegos had dropped off Martine at the apartment building and continued on to his residence. As he released his driver for the evening, he thought, "My body is tired but my spirit is invigorated by the visit with the young man." He entered his private study. A piñon-fed fire had been laid in the fireplace by his houseboy. It took the chill off the night air and filled the room with an inviting, familiar pungence. He poured a small glass of claret with one hand as he rang for the boy with his free hand. Mauro appeared silently through a huge wooden door at the other side of the room. He bowed his head in a gesture of respect.

"Si, archbishop," Mauro murmured.

"Tell Mrs. Martinez that I shall be delaying dinner for a while," the archbishop said. Remembering his cook's fiery reaction to even minute changes in household routines, he called after Mauro's already retreating shadow, "and be diplomatic when you tell her."

Producing a small key from his pocket, he opened a bottom drawer in his desk and removed a leather-bound journal. Leafing quickly through the many filled pages, he came to the first blank sheet, separated by a cardboard bookmark from those where he had traced his thoughts over the years. He never failed to note the bookmark's message, inscribed in white old English letters over a colored picture of a mountain scene of fir trees flanking a brook, threading its way through snow. The inscription was the opening verse of one of his favorite psalms: "God is our refuge, and strength, a very present help in trouble."

Crossing himself, he picked up his silver pen and scribbled the date as was his custom before each entry. The rasping pen was loud in the otherwise quiet room as he wrote: "Martine dePaul is truly a good man; he shall become a valued and trusted servant of God."

END